I0520018

SAM CRESCENT AND STACEY ESPINO

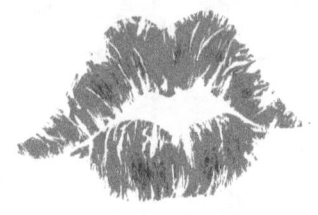

EVERNIGHT PUBLISHING ®

www.evernightpublishing.com

Copyright© 2020

Sam Crescent and Stacey Espino

Editor: Audrey Bobak

Cover Artist: Jay Aheer

ISBN: 978-0-3695-0271-1

ALL RIGHTS RESERVED

WARNING: The unauthorized reproduction or distribution of this copyrighted work is illegal. No part of this book may be used or reproduced electronically or in print without written permission, except in the case of brief quotations embodied in reviews.

This is a work of fiction. All names, characters, and places are fictitious. Any resemblance to actual events, locales, organizations, or persons, living or dead, is entirely coincidental.

SAM CRESCENT AND STACEY ESPINO

Killer of Kings, 7

Sam Crescent and Stacey Espino

Copyright © 2020

Chapter One

"I've been hit! Officer down. I repeat, officer down!"

"SWAT ... we need SWAT!"

Boss set his coffee down on the corner of his desk and rolled out his shoulders. He flicked on another monitor. He'd been following the drama for almost an hour. Normally, he wouldn't pay attention to the police scanners or live stream if it didn't involve one of his contracts, but the shootout was only two blocks away. It was past sunset and, with the streetlights out, the cops were night blind.

Although the police still had no clue what they were dealing with, he knew there were five shooters in different garages and backyards. Boss always had his finger on the pulse of the city. All five had serious firepower and were hell-bent on taking out as many cops as they could. Boss wasn't sure what was up their asses, and he couldn't care less. He stood up and strapped on a bulletproof vest and shoulder holster. He didn't plan on using a gun tonight, but he always carried.

Everyone called Boss a monster, and they were right.

Tonight, he was feeling generous.

As he readied himself in his rear gunroom, he opened the door and mobilized one of his drones, complete with heat and motion sensors. Its gentle buzzing faded into nothing once he released it into the night sky. He'd keep control with his night-vision headset. Everything he owned was state-of-the-art technology. He used his hackers to do his dirty work, but Boss was a god behind the keyboard. He never ordered a man to do anything he wasn't capable of doing himself— and that was part of Killer of Kings' success.

Lately, he'd been slacking, rarely getting his hands dirty for any of his contracts. He missed the blood, the adrenaline, the thrill of the hunt. His hitmen were the best in the world—well-trained and extremely capable— but he wanted to handle a couple of hits himself this month. Hacking, research, and surveillance didn't satisfy him on the same level as killing.

He was probably pushing fifty, but who the fuck knew. Becoming feeble and dependent on others was a deep-seated fear he rarely entertained. He'd rather eat a bullet than give up his power. So, he killed it in the gym five days a week and practiced technique and accuracy in his custom shooting range on a daily basis. No way was he going to let himself go or lose his skillset. But even the killer of kings couldn't live forever.

He took a deep breath of the cool night air once outside. Boss made his way to the shootout, keeping to the shadows. He wore all black and had a lifetime of elite training behind him. Countless lights from the police flashers colored the sky as he neared the hot zone, and intermittent rounds of gunfire cut the eerie silence. SWAT couldn't contain the scene. Numerous cops were already down, and it wasn't safe for paramedics to move in for transport.

Minutes after reaching the site, he had all his targets accounted for. It was time to pick them off, one by one. It wouldn't even be worth a phone call to get one of his hitmen to end this bullshit. Better for him to handle it himself before his coffee got cold.

He came up behind his first victim, wrapping a thick arm around the asshole's neck. Within seconds, he secured his wrist, turning his own gun on himself. Boss leaned back just enough. One head shot, and it was a suicide. With the amount of media this shitfest would inevitably get this week, he didn't want his stamp on any of it.

Unfortunately, he wouldn't be able to use his own weapons tonight.

The pungent scent of sulfur in the air irritated his senses. A negotiator's static voice sounded on the megaphone, asking the shooters to stand down. It only served to piss them off more. There were two in the next garage. Boss borrowed the gun he'd just used and struck the first guy right in the jugular. The second went in a frenzy, spraying the garage with lead, shrapnel pinging in every direction. He'd get him last because he pissed him off. After returning the gun to his first victim, he ducked down and crossed the street.

"They're firing from everywhere. Does anyone have a visible?"

Boss continued to listen in on the police communication as he handled their shit.

The next two were shooting from behind some

hedges. Anything that moved was a target. They had enough ammo to keep the party going on all night long.

What was the point of this bloodbath?

Boss's curiosity was piqued when he saw the state of his next target. He looked like shit, his heat signature off the charts. He grabbed a metal rake leaning against the side of the house, breaking off the end of the handle with his boot. As soon as the shooter stopped to reload, he moved in and punched him straight in the neck. He immediately dropped to his knees, gasping for breath. Boss dragged him by the collar and rammed his head down over the sharp end of the rake, impaling him in the neck with the jagged wood. Blood gurgled from the wound and he collapsed to the side. Another unfortunate accident. Nice and simple for the police reports.

He picked up the automatic rifle from the grass, giving it a once over before stalking the second man on this side of the street. As soon as he found him taking aim at the SWAT members running between patrol cars, Boss cleared his throat to get his attention.

"Don't shoot," he said when he saw Boss standing over him.

Boss shook his head. "I don't take orders." He pulled the trigger, spraying the man with a quick barrage of bullets. He tossed the gun and went back to handle the last punk.

The shooter was still in the same garage. The heavy darkness shrouded Boss as he moved closer. He crouched down and picked up a rock, tossing it to the opposite end of the garage. Gunfire followed the path as the guy began to panic again. Boss rushed over and knocked his feet out from under him, snatching away his weapon. With a boot on the fucker's chest, his own weapon pointing at his face, Boss chuckled.

"Last man standing. Not so cocky now, are you?" asked Boss.

"Who the fuck are you?"

"I'll ask the questions. What I want to know is why the showdown with the cops?"

The man coughed. "They're trying to kill us. *All* of us."

"Who?"

"The cops. The government. I don't fucking know."

Boss jabbed him in the ribs to keep him in line. "The guy across the street was sick. You know anything about that?"

"We're all dying off. That's their plan..." He motioned to his backpack a few feet away. "It's the drugs. That's the answer." The man cleared his throat after another coughing fit. "But they're in for a surprise. They're not just going to clean up the ghetto. Everyone fucking uses."

SWAT was moving in close. Boss ordered the drone to return to home base, then put two quick bullets in the shooter's head, dropping the gun beside the body.

Before he left, he grabbed the backpack, slinging it over one shoulder.

Fifteen minutes later, he was in the shower back home, washing away the blood and dust. It was late. His coffee was cold. He'd get some sleep and choose a challenging contract in the morning. Along with looking into what he'd discovered today. He'd never been able to let things go, not once his interest was piqued.

He washed his body, his soapy hands trailing over scar after scar. Some told stories, others were mysteries. His tattoos hid a lot of the past, but he could feel every single imperfection, his body the battlefield of a fucked-up life. Most of his history was blacked out, including his name and date of birth. According to every database, he shouldn't exist. Even he couldn't find his roots, no matter how much digging he did. The things he could remember were enough to give any man nightmares. Things were different now. He was on top and didn't make mistakes.

Boss pulled his damp hair into a low ponytail and headed to his gun room where he'd left the backpack.

His cell phone rang. "Yeah."

"Widow Maker strikes again," said Maurice.

Boss had one of his hackers track El Diablo's little sister since she'd shown up in their city. She'd proven to be a royal pain in the ass. Instead of working for him, she kept sabotaging or stealing his contracts. He should have killed her a long time ago. Her days were numbered.

"Details."

"She took Bain's latest mark, Robert Hayleigh, to a hotel. They just went in."

His jaw tightened. That asshole was as good as dead. He'd have to have a chat with Bain tomorrow. It was embarrassing having a freelancer outwit one of his hitmen. Killer of Kings had a reputation to uphold.

"I want to know exactly where she goes once she leaves the hotel."

"Will do," said Maurice.

Boss tucked his phone away.

Tomorrow was Friday.

He'd made a habit of taking a new bitch to bed most weeks. He didn't do relationships and usually tired of the same girl once she started getting fantasies of taming him. This weekend he was going to focus on a contract, so he wouldn't have time to entertain.

Unlike his men, he had better control of his cock. Boss had been dealing with romance drama for fucking years thanks to Killer of Kings. He swore he must be cursed as one after another, his hitmen fell hard for a woman. Even the most hardcore bastards ... pussy-whipped and off the market. He couldn't understand the appeal of settling down with one woman. He liked things his way, and it was a fact that emotions and loved ones were weaknesses in the underworld of contract killing.

Boss preferred everything in his life to be clean, accurate, and well-coordinated. He couldn't control what happened in his past, but Killer of Kings was a well-oiled machine with an impeccable reputation for getting the job done. He'd become the perfect assassin because he lacked empathy for his victims. Pity and second-guessing only got men killed.

He lugged the backpack onto the butcherblock counter and zipped it open. There was a large baggy of white powder among the ammunition. The shooter had ranted about drugs and being killed by a higher power. One of the men had a high fever. In addition to tailing El Diablo's sister so she didn't fuck up any more of his plans and starting a new contract tomorrow, he needed to know everything about what went down tonight.

Boss called up one of his inside men. "I need you to bring your lab and test something for me. It looks like coke, but I have a feeling there's more to it."

"I'll bring the van by. How urgent?"

"Be here within the hour. I need some fucking sleep."

****

"Please, baby, don't do it. Put it down. Let's talk about this, okay?"

Graciella set her 9mm on the glass side table with a soft clink and poured herself a glass of wine. She swirled the liquid in lazy circles, watching it cling to the sides of the crystal glass. "You like expensive things," she said, taking a sip.

"Why are you doing this?"

Robert Hayleigh's hands were handcuffed above him on the elaborate headboard. He was naked and pathetic, begging for his life. Fortunately, he was an easy mark so she wouldn't have to fuck him. Men made her sick.

She leaned back in the leather chair and continued to enjoy the wine.

He kept pleading, his fear slowing, morphing to bursts of anger. "What do you want from me, you stupid bitch? Just take my cash and fuck off."

That got her attention. Graciella stood up, her heels clicking on the marble floors of the hotel room. "Is that what you think, Mr. Hayleigh? I'm a call girl trying to rip you off?"

"You have no idea who you're dealing with," he said.

She ignored his now constant ranting. Graciella walked around the spacious luxury suite, admiring the custom woodwork. There were still fifteen minutes until her take-out order was ready at La Cocina, so she took her time. She parted the curtains and looked down at the street below, an array of lights from traffic and animated billboards illuminating the darkness. This city was her home for now. She had no intention of returning to Colombia. When she was ready, she returned to the glass table, picked her gun up, and began to twist on a silencer.

"What are you doing?"

"I'm fulfilling a contract, Mr. Hayleigh." She sat on the edge of the bed, trailing the tip of her silencer down the length of his naked body. "You'll be a good payday."

"Are you kidding me? I can't believe this shit. I'll pay you double. Triple."

"It's a tempting offer, but you've already insulted

me." She put a pillow over his head and pressed the gun to his temple, pulling the trigger.

She stared at the lifeless body for a minute, noting how numb she felt right down to her marrow. There was no sense of guilt, pity, regret, sadness. Nothing. She supposed being brutalized daily as a child had changed her into an empty shell of a woman—a walking, existing, cold-hearted bitch.

Graciella began to clean up her scene as she checked her watch. Ten more minutes until her food was ready. As she finished up, the thought of Boss's pissed-off expression made it all worthwhile. This was one of his contracts, but it was open so she'd still get paid. His men should have been faster.

She found being a female assassin to be an advantage, plus she didn't have the same strict code of ethics like Killer of Kings. Graciella would have taken Robert Hayleigh's offer of more money but she had a sore spot for assholes calling her a bitch. She would have pulled the trigger for free.

Before she stepped out into the hallway, she tugged the wavy blonde wig free and shook out her long black hair. She tucked it into her oversized purse and made her way to the elevators. The mirrored doors reflected the perfect image. That was all she was because beauty was only skin deep. She used her assets to get what she wanted, to make money, and to keep her independence. Sex was a tool in her arsenal. It meant nothing. She'd closed herself off to emotion since she was five years old. It was the last time she'd cried—the end of her innocence. For over three decades, she couldn't remember having a good night's sleep. Nightmares, real and remembered, made sure she'd never know peace. One thing she'd never sacrifice again was her freedom—she'd never allow herself to be a slave to any man.

They called her Widow Maker and she supposed the name fit her well. Killing paid well, and she was very, very good at it.

She blended into the evening crowd on the sidewalk as soon as she left the hotel. Graciella pulled out her cell phone and messaged her contact that the job was done. The money would be transferred into her account. She enjoyed collecting cash because it equaled security.

Once as she got her food and returned to her condo, she'd start a new contract. She needed to keep busy to avoid life. To avoid reflection.

It was only another block to La Cocina. She'd parked her car behind the business. Everything had been planned out in detail beforehand. No mistakes.

"Hey, gorgeous!" A few guys in their twenties stood in front of a club. She winked at them and kept walking. There was something about the night that made her feel free. The day belonged to the good girls, families, everyone without skeletons in their closets. Graciella existed on the fringe.

She passed a baby store, so she stopped and looked in the window of the closed store. Xavier, her brother, was going to have a baby in a couple of months. He'd found happiness, and that knowledge brought her a deep-seated sense of peace. She didn't blame him for what happened when they were kids.

Graciella should blame her mother. Instead, she focused her anger on all the male scum that had ripped her life to shreds. A family wasn't in the cards for her. Even a baby of her own would only ever be a fantasy, the result of a child ravaged by grown men in the most brutal way—over and over until she finally escaped as a teenager.

She pushed away the constant dark thoughts and traced a finger along the glass as she imagined the cute little outfits on her niece or nephew. Graciella had never visited Xavier since they first reconnected months ago and had no plans to. She needed to forget the past. The Graciella Moreno he knew was dead. Now she was a new woman, an assassin for hire.

By the time she got to La Cocina, her feet ached from the four-inch heels. This area was more remote, off the main street. The little family-operated take-out restaurant had become one of her favorites. Graciella loved tacos.

She picked up her order, gave a generous tip, and headed around back to her car. There were no lights in the rear, just an old dumpster and a couple of wrecked cars for parts. The food smelled delicious, and all she wanted to do was get home, shower, and eat. She set the bag and her purse in the backseat of her black Mustang Shelby, then closed the door.

A rustling caught her attention, then a knife was pressed to her throat, a beefy arm secured around her torso. "If you want to live, don't fucking scream."

She nodded and kept quiet.

He led her away from her car, shuffling her across the parking lot toward the dumpster. The man twirled her around, pressing her back against the cold metal. He held the knife against her with one hand as he fiddled with his belt with the other.

Not for one second did she feel fear.

"You don't want to steal my car?" she asked.

He didn't answer. The rapist sliced the material of her shirt, exposing her bra and a healthy dose of cleavage. She still hadn't moved.

"Good girl."

Something snapped inside her, revulsion rolling

up her spine. She'd played along long enough. In her books, there was a huge difference between a rapist and a thief.

Graciella brought her stiletto down hard on his foot and snatched away his knife so fast he probably still thought he carried it. She used the heel of her hand to his chest, knocking him back, then flipped him to the ground. With the knife under his chin, she asked. "How many women have you raped?"

"I don't know." When she didn't move the knife, he said, "None."

She laughed. Graciella got down on one knee and reached into his pants that he'd conveniently left open. "You can't rape women without a dick, can you?"

His eyes widened. One quick slice and it was over. She tossed the knife and the scrap before returning to her car. The piece of shit was lucky she left him alive.

Chapter Two

"She disappeared."

Boss gritted his teeth. "What the fuck?"

He wasn't happy.

"Look, the contract was fulfilled but I couldn't find her. Everything was done in less than thirty minutes, Boss. No one came out," Maurice said.

"She came out of the building. Get me the security footage and have your ass here now." He hung up his cell phone as he checked through the latest details of the little science experiment with the drugs. "This shit is deadly?" He looked toward his science genius.

"I've never seen anything like this before in my life. Don't get me wrong, drugs are tainted with all kinds of fillers to help bulk them out, but whatever is in here, it's killing people," Adam said. He moved across his van and started to type on his computer.

Boss rubbed at his eyes. At Killer of Kings, he didn't just have hitmen for hire. He had all kinds of men and women in his arsenal. Computer and weapons experts, doctors, gadget designers, scientists. Whatever a job called for, he had someone available to help run any given operation needed.

Adam was one of the best men he had and was willing and able to run all sorts of tests and experiments on various chemicals that came his way.

Drugs were supposed to be an easy one.

"Look, I've been tracking this thing for months, if not years. The first case of an overdose gone bad appeared about three years ago down in Colombia. It was in a bar. The kind of bar owned by a hotel. I kept the details as I figured it was more a cartel-gone-wrong kind of thing. Anyway, three months after that, at least ten people who went to the bar got admitted to the hospital all with the same symptoms. Fever, hallucinations, extreme pain."

Boss shook his head. "Why are you telling me this? It sounds like a bad case of the flu or something."

"Exactly. After this, everything goes silent until six months ago, here, in this city, ten more potential cases appear. All random. Drug dealers and users suddenly turn up at the hospital with similar symptoms. Within forty-eight hours, they're all dead. I've been thinking there's some kind of cover up to hide something, but I've got a feeling this is the real deal." Adam had this big smile on his face. "It's tainted drugs and I can tell you, whatever is the main cause in this stuff, I can't locate it. Of course, I've run all the basic tox screens, but whatever is in there is hiding."

"So this stuff is useless?" Boss asked, holding up his piece of paper. He rubbed at his temple. He was starting to get a headache. When dealing with Adam, it was always a challenge. The man got excited about chemical formulas.

All he wanted was for Maurice to arrive and give him some reprieve.

"No, it's not useless. That is the third time I've tested this stuff. This is the first, and this is the second. Look at it," he said.

Boss looked at the paperwork. "It changes?"

Adam nodded. "Yeah, it changes and believe me, I don't know how the fuck that is. I mean, it could have something to do with exposure to oxygen, heat, sweat, I don't know. This is a big deal, but this is some serious shit, Boss. You're going to need to call your contacts in the police force, because if I'm right, and this stuff is the killing coke—it means it's traveled here, and well, a lot of people are going to die."

There was a loud bang at the side of the truck.

Boss opened it to find Maurice. "I'm all set up in your office."

"Adam, I want you to put this truck into the underground parking garage and bring everything inside. I'll pay you by the hour, but I want you all over this, got it?"

"I'm expensive."

"I know. It's why I know you're the best." He left the truck and knew Adam would follow his instructions. Boss had a hunch and when he did, he always followed it. These drugs, the men tonight, the fear, the way they were, something was relevant here. He stopped at the doorway to his building and turned. Adam was already getting ready to move. "Is it airborne?" he asked.

"That I don't know, but hopefully I'll have some answers for you soon," Adam said.

"Follow protocol. I don't want you to exposed to any of this shit."

"On it."

He made his way toward his main office where Maurice had set up all the relevant security feed.

"I'm sorry, Boss," Maurice said.

"I don't want to hear it right now. Just show me what you've got." He leaned against his desk, watching the security footage of fifteen different cameras. The woman in the blonde wig, he recognized her shape and face instantly. "There she is."

She was with the target, leaning against him as if he was some kind of god. The look on her face appeared like a woman in love but he knew the Widow Maker. She was a deadly weapon.

Running a hand down his face, he watched.

"The camera by the hotel entrance. Keep it on."

About thirty minutes later, Graciella came out of the hotel room, minus the wig. She wore the same clothes but her locks were now a luscious black and a lot longer than the blonde.

"Fuck," Maurice said.

"You were watching for a blonde."

"I know. I know. I'm sorry."

"It's fine." Boss moved to his desk, opening up his laptop and accessing the cameras located on the streets. He had permanent access to the surveillance through a particular software one of his men wrote, that allowed him unlimited access to the city whenever he wanted. This was how he was able to stay on top, always follow his men, and also keep an eye on possible targets.

He watched the woman in question go to pick up some food. The sway of her hips was so sensual, he shouldn't watch, nor should he feel a stirring, but he had one nonetheless. Women shouldn't affect him, they usually didn't. Gritting his teeth, he watched her put her food in the back seat, and then there was a man in the shadows.

Boss tensed up, having to change camera angles, but the man took her down an alley that had none.

"Fuck!"

Seconds passed and Graciella came strolling out of the street as if she owned the place but he saw the look on her face. It was one of disgust. He recognized it well. There were many times he wore a similar expression.

Grinding his jaw, he waited, watching, but she left the street without another word. He watched long enough for the man who'd attacked her to come stumbling out, blood coating his pants.

It didn't take a genius to deduce she'd cut his dick off. He had to hold back a chuckle.

Sitting back, he ran a hand through his hair.

"Is that why they call her Widow Maker?"

"She has a hatred of most men," Boss said. He

didn't need to go into the backstory on this one. Graciella had been through hell. He knew every detail and it sickened him what men did to her. He also knew that most of the men involved in her kidnapping, selling, and subsequent rape were all dead.

There were gaps in the timeline he'd gathered between Graciella becoming a child sex slave to the woman she was now, a cold-hearted killer. A woman with no thoughts or feelings. If she came to work for him, he had no doubt she'd be fucking perfect at any job he set her on. He wanted her, but right now, she was causing him more problems.

"Leave," Boss said.

"I'm sorry."

"And I'm dealing with your mess. Go and assist Adam. He's going to need your help."

Once he was alone, he picked up his cell phone again and called another one of his men. "I want an address for a female, Graciella Moreno. An apartment or condo, somewhere nice, lowkey, had to have been occupied within the past few months. Send me all the data you have." He hung up and brought the image of Graciella back on his screen.

She was beautiful. A woman who could have any man she wanted but chose a life of killing for her freedom.

No one had ever been able to capture her, but she hadn't been up against the Killer of Kings before. He would find her and when he did, she was going to belong to them. She was used to being able to predict men, knowing what they wanted, but she didn't have the first clue of who she was dealing with when it came to him.

****

Sneaking into the police department was easy.

With her hair tied up, dressed all in black, she

snuck into the main detective's office, opened up his filing cabinet, and used her flashlight to read through the notes on the latest drug bust. Graciella knew Boss had been involved. It wasn't the deaths that concerned her, but the symptoms the men displayed prior to their deaths.

She had software that helped her detect certain reports with overdoses and men hallucinating, showing a fever, or flu-like symptoms. She always checked them out.

This was the fifth one in the past two weeks.

She saw the report and slammed it shut.

Fuck!

Before she left the office, she made sure there was nothing out of place. She crawled out of the bathroom window and dropped down to the pavement, only to be suddenly grabbed from behind.

"You do know breaking and entering is a criminal offense."

His voice brushed across her ear. Deep, sexy, a man in control.

She brought her elbow back and stamped on his foot. As his grip loosened, she dropped down to punch him in the gut, but Boss saw it coming and blocked. She quickly pulled back but made sure she wasn't trapped by a wall.

Her mask was still in place but seeing as they were old friends, well, more like enemies, she pulled her mask off and offered him a smile.

"You do know it's not polite to attack a girl during her work. It's not very gentlemanly."

"I'm not a gentleman. I never claimed to be." He smirked.

She noted he wasn't even in a stance to attack.

What was Boss doing here?

"Are you stalking me now? You want me to come

and work for your precious Kings? Not going to happen. I'm a lot better than they are." She'd already been paid for the last kill. Some contracts tried to renege on their deals, but she liked to put them firmly in their place. No one fucked with her. "Sloppy work on the drug bust."

"You know something about the drugs? It's why you went in there. Tell me what it is you know."

She scoffed. "I know nothing." She went to turn on her heel but Boss grabbed her, pressing her up against the concrete wall, his grip firm. She tried to pull away, but he captured her hand, locking it up tight above her head. He was stronger than she expected.

"I'm not in the mood for games," he said.

"Good, because I'm not playing."

"You've been playing games since the moment you got here. I'm not biting."

"I'd say with the way you're holding me, you're biting just enough." She smiled and his grip was suddenly around her neck.

It was odd, she wasn't afraid.

"You know, the last man to hold me like this never saw the light of day again."

"I'm not hurting you, and besides, if you really wanted to, you could get out of this. We both know that, Widow Maker."

"You've been following me?" she asked. Widow Maker. The name didn't bother her. People had a tendency to create nicknames to fit the person. She was just a woman in a man's world, doing a better job than the cock in it. Still, she didn't like how her body responded to Boss, or that she liked the thought of him following her.

No man would get beneath her skin.

"The man is going to live, if you're curious," he said.

"But he's going to do it without a dick, and every woman is all the safer."

"So you've got a thing against men? And cock?"

"I've got a *thing* against assholes who don't take no for an answer," she said. "Like, no, thank you, I'm not working for Killer of Kings."

"The offer of work was revoked. You know about the drugs," he said. "Tell me."

"I'm not talking."

She cried out as he suddenly grabbed her, jerking her forward. Instinct took over. No one manhandled her. She brought her knee up, and he blocked that. Next, she tried to pull free, but he held on to her arms. Again, he anticipated the move, and at each point of her breaking free, he knew what to expect. It pissed her off not to be in charge.

In the end, she dropped her entire body weight as if she'd fainted. He had no choice but to let go and catch her or she'd fall. The moment he did, she reacted, spinning around and putting a few feet between them. Now, she was near the entrance of the alley, and he was the one trapped.

"Interesting," he said.

She glared at him, not saying a word.

"You've got trigger points. You don't mind me grabbing your neck, or holding you in place, but if I grab you as if I'm about to drag you someplace like an animal, you can't stand it."

"You want to know about the drugs, you tell me what you've got, and I'll tell you," she said. He wasn't going to psychoanalyze her reaction. It didn't take an expert to know she was a woman with issues, but she dealt with them in her own way.

If Boss wasn't right there looking at her, she'd touch her chest. Her heart raced and not that she'd admit it to him, her hands shook a little. This reaction, this feeling, it was the first one she'd experienced in months.

"That's not the way this works."

"This is the way I work. Take it or leave it. I don't give a fuck!" She wasn't going to be bullied by men or forced into doing anything.

How dare Boss try to intimidate her.

"You know, I thought you were better than that," she said, blurting out the words before she could stop herself. She was so angry.

"What do you mean?"

"You don't care if I'm a man or a woman? Yet you used your force there to control me," she said.

He laughed. "I don't care that you're a woman. It's good to know you've still got feeling inside you somewhere."

"Fuck you." She was done with this conversation and done with him. She had more investigating to do and right now, all she wanted to do was put Boss at the top of her kill list. She turned to leave.

"El Diablo wants to see you," Boss said.

She stopped.

El Diablo.

The only real family she had left. She stopped and turned toward Boss. "I'll see him when I want to."

"You can be the biggest bitch you want, but it's not a bad move to have friends."

This made her pause. "Friends. You consider yourself my friend?"

"I could be. I'm not the worst guy in the world."

"But you're still a guy. Don't think for a second that I don't know everything there is to know about you."

"I doubt that," he said.

"The man without a past. A man surrounded in history. I'm starting to believe, Boss, that you've made yourself out to be invincible and you're beginning to believe in your own lies. It's going to get you killed. You're just a man like everyone else." She stepped toward him, feeling more herself with each passing second. Now that she had the spotlight and wasn't taken by surprise, she was in her element. Stepping up close to him, she placed a hand on his heart. "You've still got a beating heart and it's pumping blood around your body." Down she went, her hand going closer to his pants. "You could die if I were to puncture just the right artery."

"Be careful," he said.

"Even the killer of kings can't live forever."

Boss could kill her. If there was ever a man who could take her on and win, it would be this man right here. Tilting her head to the side, she watched him, waiting, and then she cupped his cock. He gritted his teeth, closing his eyes briefly.

"And you get hard like every other man." She licked her lips. "You're not invincible, Boss. You have the same desires, the same needs. All of them wrapped up in a nice little package for anyone to open." She leaned in close so her lips were right next to his ear. "I bet you love taking women. Willing of course, but I can imagine you fucking them. I bet you've broken a lot of hearts. So many women wishing to be the only thing you desire." His cock was getting hard and to her own shock, her nipples had peaked and wetness flooded her pussy. Even Boss's scent was intoxicating.

But this had to come to a stop. She wasn't here to seduce the king himself. No, she wanted answers and there were many messes she needed to clean up.

Just as quickly as she'd gotten him under her spell, she pulled back. "I've had friends, Boss. I've watched them come and go so fast. It's always interesting when it's their ass or yours, how easy it is for them to turn on you. I've experienced it all. I'm better off alone. You should know that. Nice seeing you again, and tell El Diablo I'll see him around." She took off, running in the opposite direction as far as she could.

If Boss knew anything about the drugs, then it meant they were infiltrating the city. She'd been warned about tampering with drugs years ago. So far, her one act of stupid vengeance hadn't cost too many lives, but people took drugs. She knew that. She understood the lure of a few hours of peace. If the drugs were the same ones from Colombia, then a lot of people were at risk. She'd been tracking these drugs the moment her science guy disappeared without a trace. The lab where they'd concocted this scheme had all of the formulas taken and her man was missing. What would Boss think if he knew she was the person who'd come up with the drugs that were now killing people, potentially innocent people? Possibly even kids. They did stupid shit at parties.

Pulling out her cell phone, she gritted her teeth as she dialed a number she'd promised herself she'd never, ever call. It was the one man she owed a great deal of debt to, the one man who was the complete opposite of Boss, and the only man she trusted with her very life.

Chapter Three

Twenty-four new reports in the past two days.

Boss didn't like how quickly this was spreading across his city. Fortunately, the media hadn't caught wind of it yet. Junkies overdosed. Junkies died. Only it wasn't just junkies in the hospital now. There was a politician's wife, a night-school teacher, and two fucking high school boys amongst the new numbers.

His intel guys were keeping careful track of the tainted drugs and its victims. Hospital and clinic admissions, new deaths, and underground channels were being monitored all day, every day. Anything new and he was the first to know.

He filed through the contract requests. Business was booming at Killer of Kings. All his men had one or two jobs on the go, and the backlog was growing. A few hitmen were overseas, following leads or tailing their marks. He pulled a contract that looked interesting, printing off the paperwork. Some hotshot executive had gotten himself into hot water with insider trading. He'd paid his dues, but a couple of big players were after his wife and daughter in the name of revenge. Mr. Blane Mitchell wanted them safe and wanted the men after them handled. The bounty for this contract was impressive.

Boss did some preliminary research, pulling up pics and history of the man's family. The wife was thirty-two and the little girl was ten. Cute family. Then he looked into the two killers after Mr. Mitchell. They represented two of the large companies he'd fucked over with his illegal dealings. This would require more than eliminating the muscle.

He was starting to think the payday for this one wasn't high enough after all. He'd demand more before he put in the effort.

Boss grabbed his cell.

"Maurice, I want a workup on Tyson Black and Edward Seer. I need to know their patterns over the past two weeks, firepower, family, the usual."

"Let me jot this down," he said. "Oh, by the way, Widow Maker made a local call from the lobby of her condo late last night."

"And?"

"Viko Fedorov."

Boss frowned. "Any recording?"

"We didn't have the lobby tapped. She always uses her secure cells."

"She must know we're tracking her. Why the fuck would she call him from a public place?"

"When I traced the call and saw the name, I thought you'd be interested."

"Send the bios of the men to me when you have everything," said Boss. "But Viko and Widow Maker are top priority. Get all hands on this."

He was pissed off Maurice had waited this long to tell him about the call. And why the fuck would Graciella be involved with the Circle of Monsters? The call had been local, which meant Viko was in his city. Boss didn't like to be in the dark about anything.

She must have gotten herself into trouble, or was she working for the notorious group of assassins? Either way, he planned to find out.

He wasn't sure why he cared—that woman should have been wiped off the face of the earth once she started causing problems for him. Instead, she piqued his curiosity. He found himself drawn to her. Boss was used to getting what he wanted, and right now, he wanted the Widow Maker in his bed.

Boss slammed his fist down on the desk, his

monitors rattling. He didn't like how Graciella invaded his thoughts. She was a dangerous distraction, and he had to be focused or he'd make mistakes. He wasn't following his own advice, and it had to stop. It was time to get El Diablo's little sister off his mind.

He did a little digging, called in a few favors, then messaged Killian for a ride. It wasn't Friday, but another woman was the perfect way to get Graciella off his mind. Maurice and his team would be all over this Viko Fedorov bullshit.

"Pick me up in an hour. Bring a new bitch. I feel like going out for dinner." Boss hung up and hit the shower.

Before the hour, Killian rang the doorbell. Boss finished adjusting his tie as he made his way to the front entry.

"Ready?"

"I will be in a few minutes."

Killian came in and sat on one of the armchairs, making himself at home. Although he was one of his best hitmen, he liked to use the Irish assassin as his driver most days. Trust was key in this business, and he'd taken Killian under his wing ages ago.

"You look like shit," said Killian.

Boss ignored him, checking his collar in the hall mirror. "How are the kids?"

"Growing like fucking weeds," said Killian. "I think we're going to try for another."

He scoffed. "June must have the patience of a saint to deal with you."

"She does." Killian got to his feet, brushing his unruly blond hair off his face. "What about you, Boss? What are you now? Fifty? Sixty?"

"Fuck off."

"No, seriously, you going to live alone in this

huge house forever?"

"That's the plan," said Boss. "I have enough trouble keeping up with you assholes and your family dramas."

Killian laughed. "Well, you won't want to marry the one waiting in the car, but she'll stave off the loneliness for a night."

"She cute?"

Killian shrugged. "Does it matter? She has a pussy and an ass. That's all you've ever requested, no?"

Boss slipped his jacket on over his gun holster. "Okay. I'm ready."

He secured the house and got in the back of the car. The woman waiting looked young, with dyed blonde hair and big fake tits. She smiled and reached for him.

"No touching," he warned. "Let's go, Killian. I'm starving."

He ran both hands through his hair and leaned back in his soft leather seats. These gold-digging bitches grated on his nerves. Killian was right. This fast life was going to catch up with him soon. Maybe he'd start jerking off and stay away from loose women for a while.

They pulled up in front of the restaurant, one of the most exclusive downtown locations. Boss liked the best of everything.

"Want me to hang around?"

Boss always liked to be one step ahead. Tonight would be interesting. "Yeah. Don't go too far. Keep your phone at the ready."

He walked up the main staircase with his date for the night. They passed the line outside and headed right to the hostess. Boss didn't do reservations, and he'd never had an issue.

Within seconds of being spotted by the staff, they escorted him to the exclusive part of the restaurant. He sat down across from the girl. Boss didn't know her name, and he didn't give a shit.

"Your driver said you're a business owner," said the girl.

He nodded as he flagged down the waitress for a glass of wine. One thing he wasn't interested in was a conversation with his date. He should have skipped dinner and went straight to fucking.

As he zoned out, staring at the candle lights flickering on the tables, something caught his eye. A flash of bright red. He focused for a second and immediately sat up straight in his seat. It was Graciella Moreno. At the same restaurant as him?

She did a quick sideways glance in his direction as a man pulled out the chair for her. Her sly smile was proof she'd seen him first.

"Are you okay?" asked his date.

He wanted to tell her to fuck right off, his attention riveted on the beauty a few tables over. Instead, he pushed the breadbasket in her direction and told her to eat up. It was a while later when Graciella stood up, excusing herself from the two-person table.

Boss had been monitoring them the entire night. He kept track of everything. Who the fuck was her date? Was he a mark or was this personal? He kept imagining choking the life out him, then emptying a clip into him for good measure.

Widow Maker walked in his direction. Her red dress looked like velvet, trailing all the way to her ankles, the side slit reaching just below her left hip. Her lips matched the dress, her long black hair pinned to one side with a diamond clip. Boss swallowed hard.

"Imagine finding you here," said Graciella, leaning over the table, a clutch purse in her hand. He had no doubt it carried a gun. The dress barely contained her tits as she faced him.

"Imagine," he echoed.

Graciella glanced at his date, then back to him. "Nice. Fiancée?"

"No," he said. "Just a friend."

"Aren't you going to introduce us?" Graciella asked.

Did she realize he didn't know her name? "I wouldn't want to take time away from your *date*."

She nodded. "You're right. I better get back to him before he worries."

"Nice meeting you," she said to the girl. Graciella stood up straight. "You should be careful about being so predictable, Boss. It could be your downfall." She winked and sauntered off like a fucking queen. He watched the sway of her hips, the confidence and grace in the way she carried herself. She was a true professional, and any mark would be helpless under her wiles. No doubt she'd be pissed with him tomorrow.

"Who was that?"

"Nobody."

How was he supposed to eat now? His appetite had vanished the moment he noticed her in the restaurant. He went through the motions, ordered, and picked at the food. All the while, keeping tabs on Graciella. She kept laughing at the man's jokes, touching his arm, and making sure to look over at him once in a while with those evil eyes.

Never in his life had he felt jealousy for a woman—until tonight.

****

She had Killian's car followed. Boss usually used him for transport. And she knew he'd come here.

What she didn't expect was the blonde drooling all over him.

Graciella touched up her makeup in the bathroom. She wasn't sure why she liked fucking with Boss. Maybe because he'd surprised her the other day, so she wanted to give him a taste of his own medicine. And, somehow, he made her feel safe.

Tomorrow, she had a face-to-face with Viko Fedorov. It wasn't something she looked forward to. He'd never touched her. The man was like a machine—no emotion, no bullshit. He'd insisted she do him a quick favor before the meet. Saying no wasn't an option. She had to fuck her date and provide pics so Viko could frame the married man for something.

The Circle of Monsters wasn't like Killer of Kings. Boss ran his business without a hiccup, and he had his own strict code of ethics. The Circle of Monsters were violent assassins of the underworld. They were vicious and cut-throat. And she owed Viko a major debt from years ago. He wasn't pushing her to pay up just yet, as he loved having her in his debt. She'd contacted him because she needed him to help her sort out the shit she'd started back in Colombia. Viko knew where she came from. He'd funded her little project, the one now completely out of control.

The tainted drugs were only supposed to take out the cartels who'd ruined her life. They always used their own product. But it didn't stop there. And it had mutated, getting mixed with other chemicals along the way to the US.

"Who's the suit?" Boss grabbed her arm as soon as she left the bathroom.

She gasped.

"None of your damn business," she said. "Your plaything is waiting for you. Hurry up, it's almost past her bedtime."

"I don't care about her. Who's your date?"

She rolled her eyes. "Business."

"What kind of business?"

Even with her four-inch heels, he still towered over her. He made her feel fragile and feminine, which wasn't an easy task. "The kind that pays very well."

His features were set hard. "Want me to kill him for you?"

"I'm not killing him, just fucking him."

Boss had her pressed against the wall in the hallway within seconds, his body trapping her in place. "You have skills, Graciella. Why would you sell your body for a contract?"

"It's just a body," she whispered.

They were so close. The scent of his cologne, the heat of his words, the fire in his eyes.

"I know where you come from—every detail. You deserve better than this bullshit. Cut the suit loose."

She tried to jerk out of his grip, but he was like a brick house. "You know nothing," she said. "And you don't get a say in my life."

"You can't even let your own brother into your life. You going to die a miserable, spiteful bitch?"

Graciella smacked him hard across the face.

He stared at her without reacting. Without budging.

The next moment, his lips were on hers, his hand in her hair. She closed her eyes, completely taken by the rush of passion. They kissed long and hard. The entire world went away as they devoured each other, unable to get enough. All the sexual tension between them came rushing to the surface and couldn't be contained.

She lifted her leg against his side, the slit in her dress giving her full range of motion. He grabbed her hip, grinding against her. She was completely breathless, unable to get enough of this man.

When he pulled away, she was left wanton, her entire body quaking with need. She touched her lips. Her red lipstick had to be a disaster.

"I should freshen up," she said dismissively. Graciella didn't like how much Boss affected her. He brought out too much vulnerability, in her opinion.

He caged her in with an arm to each side of her head. She wanted to feel those thick muscles for herself but fought for composure.

"Am I your prisoner now?" she asked.

Boss just stared, his jaw clenched.

"Our dates are waiting." The intimacy was more than she could handle—the look in his eyes, the fact he knew about her fucked-up childhood.

"I don't want you in his bed tonight," he said. "I want you in mine."

When Viko asked her to do something, she had to do it. Until her debt was paid in full, she had little choice in the matter. Luckily, she trusted him not to abuse her.

"I can't…"

"Why not? How much is the contract? I'll pay you," he said. "Cut him loose."

"You don't understand. I said I can't." She ducked away and disappeared into the bathroom. Emotions bubbled up because the truth was she'd much rather be in Boss's bed. A job was a job, and if she started feeling sorry for herself, it wouldn't turn out well.

He appeared in the reflection of the mirror.

"This is the ladies' room, Boss. Get out."

"Tell me why you won't let this go. You like him?"

She smirked, turning around as she leaned on the counter. "It's blackmail. My contact needs pics of him screwing a woman who's not his wife."

"Then we swap. My girl's begging to get laid. We

hook them up."

"It'll be a sad night for you then. I don't have sex for pleasure. Only for business."

"Call it whatever you want." He cupped her face, using his thumb to wipe at some of the smeared lipstick. "You're so fucking beautiful, Graciella."

Tears pricked at her eyes. God, how perfect would it be to be wanted, loved, and protected by Boss. But she'd never trust a man. Never. She could take care of herself.

"You can get any woman you want," she said.

"I can say the same thing about you. Every head turns in your direction when you enter a room."

"It's not real," she said. "This body is a guise. There's nothing under this skin." It wasn't a lie. Her confidence, her sexuality—it was all a game, all part of being the perfect assassin. The real woman was hollow, a little girl shattered into a million pieces.

"Give me one night."

She swallowed hard, tempted to take his offer, to feel like Cinderella for one night.

"You're a good kisser. But that's where this has to end." She turned, fixed her makeup, and returned to her table. Her heart raced. She wanted to go back to being the bitch, but Boss had awoken something inside of her.

Her mark wasn't bad-looking. At least she didn't have to kill him. She needed to get this over with so she'd have the pictures to give Viko tomorrow night. If she showed up empty-handed, there was no way he'd agree to help her out of this drug mess.

"I was getting worried about you," he said, reaching for her hand. She cringed but allowed it.

"Can we skip dessert?" She bit her lip slowly, sensually, to show her intention. He took the bait, immediately requesting the check. Graciella didn't even bother to look at Boss or his sexy little plaything again. She ducked out with her date, and they walked out to the lot to find his car. She was anxious to get the hell out of there.

The sound of burning rubber made them both look up. A car raced down the street, braking right in front of them. It was dark out, only a few streetlights helping them to find their way. Killian leapt out of the driver's seat, leaned over the top of the car, and aimed a gun.

"Back off, Widow Maker."

"What is this?"

The second she stepped away from her date, and he was shot dead, his body collapsing to the ground. Killian saluted with the gun, gave her a smirk, and then sped off down the road.

"You've got to be kidding me." He didn't have to die, even if he was a cheating bastard. She stepped over the body and headed back to the restaurant.

Her feet were killing her. She stormed through the tables, ignoring the staff asking where she was heading. Boss smiled and raised a glass of wine as she approached his table.

"Who do you think you are? You've just screwed this up for me."

"Don't know what you're talking about, sweetheart."

"Yeah, Killian was just acting out on his own, right?"

Boss shrugged. "Then you shouldn't have brought your date to the same restaurant you knew I'd be at. I'd say you were asking for this to happen."

She had no clue why she'd arranged it like this, but she couldn't go back and undo it. Sometimes she couldn't even understand her own actions. But she had major explaining to do tomorrow with Viko, and her stomach already felt queasy thinking about it.

"You're an asshole," she said.

He set down his glass and waved for the waitress. "Put this on my tab and call a cab for the young lady."

"But—"

Boss put a finger to his lips to silence the girl's protests.

Graciella couldn't understand why she felt so much satisfaction when Boss blew off his date. The girl wasn't happy, ready to stomp and pout.

He got up and headed to the front of the restaurant by himself. Graciella followed after him. Once they were alone and out of earshot of everyone, she grabbed his sleeve. "What gives you the right?"

Boss stopped and faced her, not intimidated in the least. "I didn't want to share you."

"I'm not yours to claim."

Chapter Four

I'm not yours to claim.

The words echoed through Boss's mind as he started to moan. What the fuck had happened last night? One moment he'd been getting under Graciella's skin, the next total darkness. He couldn't even remember what he'd said afterward.

Lifting his arms up, he became aware of the clinking of metal. Glancing down, he groaned. What the fuck?

As he became more alert, he realized he was on a bed with chains around his wrists. "Fuck!"

Touching his body, he found that he still had his clothes on but his cell phone, guns, and knives were all gone.

He couldn't recall much from the previous night. That was some strong shit.

"It is a rare occurrence indeed to conquer the great Boss of Killer of Kings."

Boss turned to see Viko sitting in the corner of the room, looking calm and relaxed.

"Your handiwork, I suppose," he said.

"I couldn't resist the chance. I mean, you really did make it so easy."

He glanced around the room. No sign of the Widow Maker. "Was I the mark?"

Viko clucked his tongue. "You know, I admire you. You are such an excellent marksman. You're the boss of your entire empire, but you really shouldn't allow a woman to distract you so easily."

The television across the room came to life and he saw Graciella lying on a bed. The red dress she'd worn had been removed. She was completely naked and he saw men in the room, waiting.

"You leave her the fuck alone!" Boss couldn't contain his rage.

He and Viko were a lot alike. They both had their own organizations to run, but Boss had morals, ethics, a little of them anyway. Viko always had his own agenda. Where Boss could walk out in the day, be seen on cameras, Viko had to keep to the shadows. He was a wanted man in most countries, but no one could find him. He lived a life of luxury, leaving death and decay in his wake.

"Where's Killian?"

"Oh, don't worry about him. I'm sure he's rounding up your men as we speak."

"What is this about?" he asked. "You wanted an audience with me, you ask for it, you don't do it like this."

"Boss, I do what I like when I like. Now, I've seen the way Graciella has made you behave these past few months. She has certainly gotten under your skin. I gave her a job, and I expected it done to the best of her abilities. She's amazing at what she does. I don't have personal experience with this, of course."

"You know she was raped as a child. Hurt over and over again," Boss said.

"I know her story. It's why I never killed her. You see, Boss, what you need to understand is I'm the hero of her story. You want to know who helped her? I did. When it comes to her, she is somewhat … like a pet that I just can't seem to want to kill."

Boss glared at him. "Then why are those men with her?"

"Oh, Boss, you really need to get a grip. Graciella is a deadly weapon. I can't keep her here unless she is completely naked. It's the way we work, unless we meet in public circumstances. The men have dealt with her before, and she is known to snap necks if they even so much as touch her inappropriately."

"I was the one who killed her mark," he said. He had to protect her. Whatever it was that Viko had given him, it was making him very fucking sick.

"I know you killed the cheating scumbag. He didn't need to die, you know. I mean, I was going to kill him because he didn't intend to pay but sometimes I like playing with the men. Just so you know, Graceilla wouldn't have actually had sex with him." Viko shrugged. "She'd have worked him up, made him pass out, took the necessary photographs that showed what needed to be seen, and then he'd have woken up with no memory but a beautiful naked woman by his side. She only uses her body if she has to. It's the one area where she is a master, but I'm afraid no man has ever been able to show her how good it can be." Viko got to his feet. "I'm bored of this conversation." He threw the keys at Boss. "Join us when you're free."

Boss didn't even hesitate unlocking his cuffs and marching toward the door. He stopped, checked the room, and he found what he was looking for. A gun had been left. He picked it up, checked the chamber, and left the room.

He followed the sound of Viko's voice and pointed his gun, only to come to a stop when he saw Graciella sitting at the dining room table, two guns poised at her head, and she was still completely naked.

Her gaze was on him and he watched as she shook her head.

Poor thing had no idea.

"We can do this the easy way or the hard way, Boss. I don't really care which. Just know that you brought this on yourself. We can work together or I can kill you. I honestly don't mind which it is. I'm game for anything. This is my kingdom though and I don't take to having a gun pointed at me lightly."

He lowered the gun, putting it on the floor.

"Excellent. Now that we know Graciella isn't hiding anything, we can get her a robe," Viko said. "You care to join us, Boss? The drugs I used will wear off even faster with food." Viko picked up a piece of orange and placed it in his mouth. "Dig in. There's plenty of food to go around."

Boss didn't expect Graciella to dig in but she did as soon as she had a robe. He watched her eat with relish, not once looking toward Viko.

"Am I the only person here with any sense?" Boss asked.

"I'm not going to kill you, Boss. You can eat without worrying."

"I don't want to eat. I want to know what all of this is about."

"Eat," Graciella said. "It's not polite to ignore offered food."

He didn't pander to anyone's needs but he did need food. The drugs he'd been given to knock him out had lingered a little too long for his liking. Picking up some fruit, he took bites, being careful and clocking all the available exits and possible difficulties he'd have.

"So, we have a problem. The drugs," Viko said.

Graciella paused. "You know."

"Of course, I know. I've been tracking them ever since the formula went missing, as did our chief scientist."

Boss looked at the two of them. "What do you know about the drugs?"

"That they've crossed the border and are leaving a trail of bodies," Viko said.

"I've got to clean the mess up," Graciella said.

"You know why."

Boss didn't like this. "You know about the drugs? The fever? The reactions? The hallucinations?"

Graciella looked at him and nodded.

"This is your time to speak up, Graciella," Viko said.

"I've had enough of your fucking voice!" Boss growled. With each piece of food he consumed, his rage built. He hadn't let himself be taken in a long time. Being at the mercy of anyone was against everything he stood for. He was the one who went and got his men to safety, not the other way around.

"Be careful," Viko said.

"I'm the one who created the drugs," Graciella said.

"You didn't create them, dear. She was the one with the idea. I just thought it was brilliant, and so I funded and helped to see through to fruition."

"It was only supposed to be for the cartels. The ones who dealt in flesh and blood. Who steal boys and girls and destroy them," Graciella said. "I made a promise to myself during my captivity that if I ever got the chance to kill them, I would. Only, they deal in drugs, and I knew they sampled their own product. The idea was to make a batch that was tainted. The men would die a painful death, but I'd get all of them quickly. They had celebratory parties."

"It went wrong," Viko said. "Our facility was ransacked. The scientist involved disappeared along with the product. We believe he stole some of the formula and has been working to branch it out."

"Wait, hold on a minute. You're telling me the drugs that are now killing people came from you?" Boss asked. "Why would they sell this shit if it's killing people?"

"I guess they thought they might have been able to change it, I don't know. I'm not a scientist. I don't know how this works," Graciella said. "It's why I've come to you." She turned to Viko. "We've got to stop this."

"I warned you, Widow Maker, that you'd make a move you'd regret. Every single death is on your hands."

"Now wait just a minute," Boss said.

"I have my sources looking into this. Your debt to me just doubled, Graciella. Know this, you will be indebted to me for the rest of our life. After last night, you better hope you don't fail me again."

****

Graciella paced in Boss's office. The room was massive. This wasn't how she wanted this to go down. She'd hoped to be able to deal with the drug problem herself but now it was taken completely out of her hands, and she didn't know what to do.

He'd been so angry with her.

It doesn't matter. Whatever he thought about her, she'd deal with it.

The drugs had been a stroke of genius when she had control of them. Now, they were a royal pain in the ass. With Viko helping as well, she didn't know if having the Circle of Monsters involved would be a good idea.

Boss finally arrived and any remains of the drug he'd been given were gone. She'd been given the same drug. The side effects weren't exactly refreshing. She liked to be in control at all times, and being drugged put her in a bad place.

He wasn't alone as he entered the office. Killian, Bain, and El Diablo all entered.

She looked at her brother. A part of her wanted to run into his arms and pretend the last couple of decades hadn't happened, but she wasn't a little girl anymore.

Hadn't been for a long time. He couldn't help her fight the demons that plagued her every single day of her life. Pushing her hair off her face, she was very aware of the fact she still wore the robe Viko had given her.

Being naked in front of men didn't affect her. She'd long gotten over the fear and worry of being near a man. Viko didn't trust her but then, she'd never really given him a reason to trust her.

"Graciella," he said.

"El Diablo." She rarely called him by his given name and she knew it pissed him off. He gritted his teeth.

"You're not keeping out of trouble?"

"I have a problem with finding trouble." She shrugged.

"Enough. Tell me it worked," Boss said.

She looked at Boss then at Killian.

"It worked. We can hear him and we know where he's going to be and when."

"What exactly is going on here?" Something was going on and she didn't know what. She hated being kept out in the dark.

"Do you want to tell her?" Boss asked.

She turned to her brother.

"You don't really believe Viko got the better of Boss?"

She looked toward Boss. "You planned this."

"All down to the little details of being captured."

Killian shrugged, a guilty grin on his face. They were all in on this bullshit.

"So the little whore you were with, that was all part of the plan?" she asked. She hated how jealous she sounded. Not that it mattered to her what Boss was doing or with whom.

"She was just a little fun. What we've got now though, that is what's important," Boss said.

"It all was a lie."

Fuck, she couldn't believe this. She actually believed Viko had outsmarted Boss. She should have known better.

"I'm always one step ahead of you, Widow Maker. You shouldn't underestimate me."

The fact Boss had been working on his own plan pissed her off even more. She'd been played, kept out of the loop, and no one did that to her.

"Well, I see you have everything in order. You don't need me." She walked toward the door only for her brother to step in her way. "Move."

"You're upset."

"You don't know me, brother. You don't know what I'm capable of. Move." She snapped the last word, but he shook his head. "I'll hurt you."

"Then hurt me. I promised to protect you."

"And you fucked that up," she said.

He jerked as if she'd slapped him. "But I can protect you now."

"Ask your boss if I need protecting. I don't need any man."

"You need to tell us about the drugs, Graciella," said Boss.

One moment it was Widow Maker, the next Graciella.

"Do you realize what you've done?" she asked. "You think Viko doesn't know?"

"I'd say with the fact he's got two women with him and he's fucking them into oblivion, I'd surmise he doesn't know."

She shook her head. "You have to agree to work with Viko."

"I don't work with anyone like him."

She growled. "You're going to get yourself and

everyone killed. Do you realize that? Do you have a clue how dangerous this all is?"

"Killian, Bain, Xavier, leave."

"I'm not leaving," said Xavier.

"I need to talk to my guest alone."

"How about I leave and then you can deal with whatever shit you've got going down. You don't need me," she said.

Boss ignored her.

The men left, one by one until she was alone with Boss once again.

"You should know by now I always have a plan to get what I want. I'm meticulous when it comes to details. I don't make mistakes."

"I don't have to listen to any of this crap." She crossed her arms over her chest.

"Those drugs are killing innocent people. I had no idea you were the one responsible. You need to tell me what you know."

She'd been heading for the door but she whirled around to scream at him. "You know everything I know. I haven't got some secret I'm hiding from you."

"Really, what about the fact you were the one responsible for bringing the drugs into this in the first place?"

"It was a big fucking mistake. I know that now. You think I want innocent people to die? I don't. I mean, they can't be so innocent if they're taking drugs." She needed to be cold, to not think and feel. "I don't have to justify my actions to you."

"You're right, you don't, but this is going to be a shitstorm. Cases are increasing, Graciella. People are dying."

"I'm handling it."

"By going to men like Viko?"

"He's not as bad as he seems," she cried out. "Why am I even justifying these actions to you? I don't need to explain any of this. I made a decision years ago and it has come to bite me in the ass. I don't need you or your men, I'll handle it."

"Like you handled your mark last night?"

She took a step toward him. "Be careful. That was the only time you get to fool me, Boss. Do not mistake me for some kind of damsel. You crossed the line. I don't want anything to do with you."

He grabbed her arm as she made to leave, capturing her close.

"If you come and work for me, you wouldn't ever need to use your body. You would be safe."

She shook her head. "You're wrong, Boss. This is the worst kind of business to be in. I know that, you know it. I'm going to end up dead like all of my other marks. My days are numbered and after everything I've done, a quick death would be a mercy to me."

"You're not dying."

"Look at my record. I've killed so many people. The drugs, you think that is the worst thing I've done? It's not. From the moment I was taken, I was lost. I'm not a good person."

"If you're not a good person, why are you trying to locate the source of the drugs? That was why you broke into the police department, wasn't it? You wanted to determine if the drugs were back? Is that why you're still here? Or is there another reason?" he asked.

He was so close.

His lips—all it would take was her to lean in and she'd kiss him.

She'd always hated kisses. They were normally wet and disgusting, giving way to a man's need. Boss's kiss hadn't been gentle or fumbling. He knew what he was doing and he'd taken complete control. It was the first and only kiss in her life she'd really enjoyed.

Viko had once made her kiss him. That had been one of the payments he'd required. A single kiss. It was many years ago, but the one she'd given him made her feel nothing. Boss made her feel and she couldn't have that.

"What's the matter, Boss? Do you think I've come to stick with you? That you can hold all of my attention?" She pouted. "I'm here to do a job and when it's done, I'm out of here."

"I could kill you," Boss said. "If that's what you're hoping for."

She shook her head. "I don't want to die."

"You're not really living."

"Look around you, I can do whatever I want."

"You go home alone every single night, eat takeout, watch movies. You're telling me you're not lonely?"

"Takes one to know one, Boss." She pulled out of his arms. "Stay away from me."

"You're not going anywhere," he said.

"You can keep at your desk, going through the same old bullshit reports all you want, but the real answers come from ground work. That's what I'm going to be doing." She opened his door and was gone. She didn't immediately leave. Boss's office was full of weaponry and clothing. She went to one of the supply closets and found some sweatpants and a shirt in her size. She'd just finished getting dressed when El Diablo came in. He stood at the doorway, his arms crossed over his chest.

"You don't have to keep on running," he said.

"I don't have time for the brotherly rant."

"Damn it, Graciella. I want us to be a family."

She flicked her hair out from her shirt. "We'll always be a family. We're just not going to be the kind that share postcards and Christmas gifts. We're just a brother and a sister by blood."

"You know not a day went by when I didn't think about you," El Diablo said.

She shrugged. "And I guess it didn't work out too badly for you. I'm not doing this with you, Xavier." She spoke his name, hoping to hurt him enough for him to shut up and let her leave.

"I don't want you to go," he said. "Let us help you."

"I got into this mess and I'll find a way out of it. It's what I'm good at." Someone had a main lab. She had to locate it, destroy it, kill the fucking scientist and every single person who was in on the distribution, and then remove all of the product. Piece of cake, just so long as she stayed away from Boss, she'd be fine.

Chapter Five

He dropped the file folder on the corner of his desk. "Don't fuck this one up," Boss said.

Bain groaned and snatched the file.

"How was I supposed to know that bitch was tailing my mark?" Bain said.

Boss cringed. "Don't call her a bitch."

Bain narrowed his eyes but kept his mouth shut. He leafed through the folder. "Piece of cake." He kept tugging at his collar, and Boss noticed sweat beaded on his forehead.

Boss cocked an eyebrow. "You feeling okay?"

"What?" Bain was a cold motherfucker. He'd had a hellish childhood, but now he was happily married. He deserved it. Boss personally invested himself in the people he invited to work for him. Killer of Kings was more than just a group of hitmen. It was much more than the Circle of Monsters.

"Nothing. Call me when it's done."

Once Bain left, he sat in his office chair and tapped a pen against his lips. After everything that had gone down last week, the one thing that kept lingering in his mind was the fact Graciella thought he should be afraid of Viko. She was massively in debt to the fucker and believed he was some kind of god. It pissed him off that she hadn't come to him first.

He wanted to be her hero.

Little did she know the extent of Boss's power. The Circle of Monsters didn't give him pause. This was his city. Killer of Kings ruled these streets.

His cell rang.

"What is it, Maurice?"

"She's on the move."

Of course, she is.

He'd asked a couple of his men to keep tabs on Graciella's movements. Not just for information on the drug shitstorm she'd started, but for her own damn good. Maybe more. "Where?"

"She's driving. Heading out to the beach."

"The beaches?"

"Area looks deserted. Just a few structures up ahead. She's slowing down." After a couple of minutes, he continued, "Okay, I'm sending you the address. She's gone inside."

"Good work. I'll head out there now."

"Want me to send Killian or Chains with a car?"

"No, not this time. Find out where Tyson Black will be tonight. I'll be paying him a visit." Boss hung up.

Was Graciella meeting Viko? Was she hiding something? Whatever it was, he'd find out soon. With the Widow Maker on his mind, he couldn't focus on his contract just yet. He put the address into his software, zooming in on the dilapidated cabin. Her car was parked out front. For a city girl living in an upscale condo, he doubted she enjoyed slumming it.

It was in the middle of nowhere. No other cars in sight. He waited for his satellite to scan the house for heat signatures. She was alone. His curiosity was piqued, and that was rarely a good thing.

He headed to his weapons room and strapped himself with firepower. He'd had enough of masquerading as the victim last week, and he had no plans on repeating it. Boss drove out to the beaches, rolling down his window as the paved roads turned to dirt. The air smelled different out here, salty and fresh. Seagulls cawed and he could already hear the waves before he saw them. He crested a low dune, and then he saw the old wooden cabin. It looked lonely and weather-beaten. The waves were rough, crashing on the shore, creating a flurry of white wash.

As he slowly rolled toward it, his sensors went off on his dash. Interesting. He'd been picked up on surveillance. This wasn't the first time she'd come here. What was she up to? He kept driving. The Widow Maker already knew he was there, so there'd be no surprise visit today.

Maybe she'd planned this and wanted to assassinate him. He supposed there were worse ways to go.

He parked his car and walked up to the front door, the old floorboards on the porch creaking with each step. Boss didn't knock. He turned the handle and pushed open the door. The second after the gun rested against his left temple, he'd twisted her arm and taken it away.

"What the fuck?" she said, holding her wrist.

"Is that how you welcome guests?"

"Guest? As far as I'm concerned, you're breaking and entering. Don't you know how to knock?" she asked.

He walked in, tossing her gun on a low dresser. Boss checked out the small, open-concept cabin. It was a lot more presentable inside than out. There was a double bed, nightstand, dresser, and oversized wicker chair with a big floral cushion. It didn't look like Widow Maker's style. "What is this place?"

"None of your business."

He shrugged. Boss never expected a straight answer from her. She was the most difficult female he'd ever dealt with. "This where you fuck your marks?"

"Bastard." She lunged at him and he grabbed both her wrists. He loved pushing her buttons. There was something deeply satisfying about toying with Graciella.

"You should really learn to control that Latina temper of yours. It'll be your downfall."

"Funny how you're the only one who manages to

piss me off." She struggled to free her arms but she wasn't going anywhere until he decided so. "What do you want from me now?"

"I want to know why you drove all the way out to this piece-of-shit cabin. You're hiding something."

She shook her head. "What you see is what you get. I'm not hiding anything."

"You met with Viko a few days ago. Don't forget I'm watching him. And you. What did you talk about?"

Graciella huffed. "Why don't you ask him yourself?"

"I thought I'd ask you. He's your master, after all. Like he said, you'll be in debt to him for the rest of your life. That what you like? Being a slave to a man like him?"

Her eyes narrowed, but that was all the emotion he could get out of her. He knew he'd hit a sore spot, but she managed to keep up her iron walls.

"You like being put on show for piece-of-shit assholes like Viko? He said that wasn't the first time he's had you stripped naked."

"So what? I've told you before it's only a body."

"And I've told you you're better than this."

Her figure was fucking perfection. Thick thighs, rounded hips, and a killer ass. She filled out everything she wore in an unholy way. And she knew exactly how she affected men. Graciella was the whole package. Only she wasn't. Her beauty was skin-deep, the rest a dark abyss of pain she lived to keep buried. Boss was convinced he was the only man who could handle a woman like her.

But he wasn't looking to settle down. Not now. Not ever.

Only the distant sound of waves and their combined breathing could be heard. They were so close.

"You came here for a reason," she finally said.

"I don't like secrets. Yours tend to be deadly."

"Again, I didn't plan on this happening," she said. "And I'll clean everything up. I'm working on it."

"Where does this cabin come in?"

She exhaled. "It's mine, okay? A place I like to come to sometimes. It helps me think."

Even the heartless Widow Maker needed an escape. Boss never granted himself such liberties. Too dangerous.

"You like the ocean?" he asked. Graciella was cold, calculating, and ruthless. Discovering she had hidden passions was worth the drive out to the beach.

She didn't answer him, but he expected no less.

"Mind if I have a seat?"

"Make yourself at home," she said, snatching her hands away once he relaxed his grip. He sat on the edge of the bed, the springs squeaking slightly from his weight.

"I never thought of you as a floral girl," he teased.

"You know so little about me, Boss. You think you know everything, but you can never get in here." She used two fingers to tap her head.

"I want in there."

She sauntered toward him, standing directly in front of where he sat. Her legs were bare. She only wore a short white sundress, and it highlighted her golden skin. "You get everything you want, don't you?" she asked.

"Almost."

He ran both his hands up the backs of her legs. She didn't flinch away.

Boss groaned, his cock already stiff and uncomfortable.

"Have you had many dinner dates lately? I'm

sure you can have any woman you want. You're the great Boss of Killer of Kings, after all."

"No dates. And the only woman I'm interested in right now is already here."

"Now I'm the conquest of the week. I suppose I should be flattered."

"You should," he said.

"I guess I'm good for one night," she said. "But men like you don't settle for women like me. You want virgins. Young, sweet things to balance out the darkness. I know how it works," she said.

"What happens to women like you?" he asked. There was pain in her words. He wasn't used to getting an emotional response out of the raven-haired beauty.

"We become forgotten. Lost. Nobody really cares about the broken ones."

His hands drifted higher up her thighs. Fuck, her legs were smooth. He felt the edge of her panties.

"I'm not most men. And, sweetheart, a virgin would never be able to handle me."

****

Graciella had come here specifically because she knew Boss would follow. She hated the fact he'd outsmarted her last week with Viko. She couldn't get him off her mind.

There was no way she'd admit she was in way over her head. There was only so much Viko could or *would* do to help her. Knowing Boss was invested in ending the drug problem was like having an insurance policy, and it brought her a measure of comfort.

She rested her hands on his shoulders. Seducing men was her specialty, but touching Boss was no ordinary day on the job. He was hard and corded with muscle, a beast of a man. He alone brought out her vulnerabilities and she hated it.

"What's your real name?" she asked.

He smirked.

"You know mine."

"I have no name," he said.

His tone made her want to take back the question. She didn't pry further.

"How'd you get this scar?" He traced an old scar on the front of her thigh. His big hands on her legs sent skitters racing all the way to her pussy, but no way would she let him know how much his touch affected her.

"We'll be here all night if you ask about my scars. I have too many to count. And most of them have stories I'm not interested in revisiting."

"You're not the only one."

Boss let go of her legs and shrugged off his jacket. He was strapped with weapons. She was surprised when he slid his holsters off and set them on the nightside table. It wasn't like him to be off guard. When he pulled off his t-shirt, tossing it on the bed, her breath caught.

"Try and count them." He winked.

His body was covered in ink, rock hard and ripped. And he was right. There were scars littered all over his body. Much worse than hers. God, she wanted to touch him, but Graciella had never allowed herself to become emotionally invested in a man. Boss was the only one capable of changing that. What was happening to her?

She knew firsthand the type of man he was. Boss fucked different women every week, and she knew that for a fact. Graciella had been attempting to watch his movements for months. It wasn't easy. The man was like a ghost. Each time she saw him pick up different women, it gutted her, and she envisioned herself in their place.

Only she would never be his disposable

plaything. That was all a killer like Boss was interested in.

She swallowed hard and got to her knees in front of him. This was the role she played—the seductress, the Widow Maker. It ensured she'd never be a victim. She smoothed her hands over his chest, shoulders, and along his arms. His scars weren't a turn off. They were part of him, part of a wicked past. They showed he'd survived—same as her.

He cupped her face and leaned over to kiss her. She attempted to back away, but it happened fast. She kissed him back, savoring the fullness of his lips and domination of her mouth. He even tasted good, a mix of mint and raw masculinity. Boss lifted her sundress up over her head, leaving her in just a pair of lace panties.

Could she keep her heart out of this? Should she back out before it was too late?

Part of her wanted to seduce, another part, a new untapped part, wanted to be ravaged. She'd never given in to a man, never allowed herself to become seduced or enjoy sex. Everything was business, and if things ever got personal, she knew it would destroy her. Her past would never allow her to have a normal relationship. The horrific memories would no doubt show up and ruin things, or worse, make her weak and helpless.

"Come here, baby."

She straddled his lap, slowly, deliberately, feeling his hard-on through his dark jeans as it rubbed against her pussy. Graciella had to stifle a gasp. It felt so damn good. She wriggled, wanting to affect him the same way.

"Is Killian waiting outside?"

He shook his head. "It's just you and me."

Boss kissed her jaw, his stubble scraping her skin. His hands cupped her ass, pulling her closer. He was so strong and in control. She wrapped her arms around his neck and closed her eyes, allowing herself to enjoy his attention. Having the great Boss in her bed was indeed an accomplishment. She'd never had such a powerful man interested in her. Even Viko never cared to touch her.

She should use this opportunity to her advantage, to wrap him around her finger. Graciella craved control, to have the upper hand. But was that even possible with Boss?

"What are you going to do with me?"

He smirked. "Make you love me."

She ran her hand through his thick hair, examining his face, the crinkles at the corners of his eyes and the intensity as he stared at her. "You're wasting your time. That's not possible."

He rose slightly, twisting her body onto the bed so he dominated. Boss stared down at her, hunger in his eyes. If she didn't know men so well, she'd swear he was about to kill her. His dark eyes were always cold and flat, like a man without a conscience. He was so hard to read.

"I've always loved a challenge." He kissed her neck, trailing kisses down between her breasts, then over her stomach. Her body quivered. When he reached low enough, she braced herself, holding her breath. But he used a knee to lift himself up and stood at the edge of the bed.

She released the breath, her pulse racing.

"The offer's still open if you want work." He put his t-shirt on and started strapping on his holster as she lay there half-naked on the bed, her pussy still pulsing.

Was he even human? She knew damn well he'd had a hard-on for her.

Graciella leaned up on her elbows. "What the hell are you doing?"

He smirked, a barely-there evil smirk.

She leaned over and grabbed her dress off the

floor, quickly pulling it on to cover herself. She absolutely hated how small he made her feel. "Couldn't go through with it? Let me guess, the thought of other men fucking me was too much of a turn off."

He just stood there, quiet, unmoving, staring down at her.

"I'm just a dirty whore, right?"

This time, he inhaled and narrowed his eyes. His intensity would make most men piss themselves.

"First of all, I don't fuck unwilling women. Your body says you're ready, but you're not. Secondly, once I do claim that body, and I will, no other man will have the pleasure again. I'll have to consider killing everyone who's ever touched you once you're mine."

"That'll be a full-time job."

His rejection stung. A frog grew in her throat. What was he doing to her? Why couldn't he just screw her like everyone else she seduced? It would have given her power and enabled her to play him for inside information. She was good at her job and never thought twice about using every situation to her advantage.

This was different.

No matter how hard she tried to push him, he never took the bait. He was trying to toy with her, make her feel special when she wasn't. Boss didn't take women seriously, so if she thought she was different, she was a fool.

"You should really stop thinking so low of yourself. I don't judge people by their pasts. Give yourself a break, Graciella." He headed to the door. She wanted to beg him to stay, to continue what they'd started, but he was right. About everything.

She was pulling at straws now. "How would Xavier feel about you coming to my cabin?"

He scoffed. "El Diablo works for me. Not the

other way around."

Then he was gone.

She touched her lips, his kiss still lingering.

Once he drove away, his car completely off her radar, her cell phone went off.

"Have a nice visit?"

Viko had once been her savior, now, not so much. She knew exactly where she stood when it came to him. As long as she was useful or in debt to him, he tolerated her.

"Why are you watching me?"

"I've thought of a way for you to pay off your debt to me."

She sat up straighter, adjusting the phone. "How much?"

"All of it."

Graciella swallowed hard. One of the hardest things she had to deal with in her adult life was being in debt. She hated being at the mercy of anyone, especially a man like Viko Fedorov.

"I'm listening."

"Kill him."

"Who?"

He laughed, the sound crawling up her spine. "Who else? The killer of kings."

Chapter Six

A couple of hours later, Boss sat in Viko's chair. The man had a nasty cigar habit. After cutting up the expensive, pretentious smokes, he sat back, dirty boots on the desk, and waited. After a short time, his cock had finally gone down, but he had a feeling that was more due to his persistence in thinking about bad shit than actually taming his own arousal. When it came to Graciella, he didn't think straight. She made him want so many things.

He had no doubt in his mind that if he wanted to, he could have fucked her hard and fast, even got her close to coming, but she expected that. She'd tensed up. Her body screaming for him to stop, even while her lips remained closed. He hated it. The only way he would ever take Graciella to bed was when she was ready.

Graciella didn't realize it yet, but they were connected. He didn't know the whys of it. No woman had ever held his attention long enough for him to give a shit. There was something different about her and it wasn't her ability to fight either, although that was a huge attraction. She could handle herself but he detected a vulnerability. No one had taken care of her, showed her love—not without a price.

What he needed to do first was gain her trust. Allow her to see the real him.

Between the drugs, Graciella, his contracts coming in, Viko, and plenty of other shit he was sure waited at his desk, he certainly wasn't bored.

Viko entered his office, flicking on the light. His guards tensed up the moment they caught sight of him. Boss didn't budge.

"Breaking and entering is illegal," Viko said, looking somewhat unimpressed.

"Yeah, and I find issuing out a death contract on my head a little rude." To add to his insult, Boss pulled out his gun and fired two bullets, taking out both of Viko's guards. They didn't even get a warning shot. He also had a suppressor on to keep things quiet.

Viko tutted. "I'm an opportunist. You think I don't see your fascination with her?"

Boss got to his feet. "You're in my town and you think you can continue to insult me?" He rounded the desk, gun at his side, waiting. "I could put a bullet in your head and no one would even mourn you."

Viko smiled. "Yeah, but there's a reason you and I are still standing. Where you keep your assassins in line, we both know I keep the monsters at bay."

Boss chuckled. "You seem to think that my men are what, tame? They're babies? They do as they're told."

"Everything you guys do is based on a contract. You're all good boys. You have a nice little office. State-of-the-art technology. Everything with you is clean and quick. You don't even know what hunts you in the darkness."

He scoffed. "Viko, you're a fool. It's why you always have substandard men. You don't control anyone. The money is what makes your world go round. I want you out of my city, tonight. You stay, the next time I see you, I'll put a bullet in your brain."

"Graciella will kill you," Viko said.

Boss smiled and looked toward his enemy. "No, she won't. You and I both know it's an empty threat. I know you, Viko. By knowing you, I look at the little details not many people would. You like Graciella. By making sure her debt to you is never repaid, you can keep an eye on her."

"You're turning soft in your old age."

"No, I'm not. I do my research. You never have any outstanding debt. They pay up, or they're dead. You've left a trail of bodies in your wake, all of them indebted to you, but Graciella mysteriously wanders through life unscathed. Now, I don't think you're in love with her, but you admire her. She's like a daughter you never had. She's strong and you're invested in her future, and you also know there are limits to what she will do. Right now, she's focused on cleaning up her mess, not killing me."

"You think you know everything," Viko said. "You know nothing."

"I know enough. I didn't know about her existence. You did. You saved her when I couldn't. That is what's keeping you alive." Boss left.

Killian waited for him outside. After climbing into the car, Killian drove off.

"I thought I told you not to wait."

"You did, but I also don't mind disregarding orders. We all may hate you most of the time at Killer of Kings, but you're still a good guy deep down."

Boss looked sideways at him. Killian was a good man, but he didn't believe the bullshit coming from his mouth. "Did you plant a device on me?"

"Nope. You've got some major trust issues, Boss. I figured you'd need some backup. Viko is not a man to mess with."

"And you think I am?"

"He's the first guy you've put yourself at the mercy of. It may have all been an act, but I'm not stupid. I know the real risks at play, and so do you. If Viko wanted you dead, you'd be dead."

"This is a vote of confidence?"

"You and Viko are evenly matched. This is just a dick-measuring contest between the two of you. Why do you want him out of the country and if so, what does Xavier's sister have to do with this?"

"I don't have to give you my reasons."

"Look, I hate to break it to you, but seeing as the drugs and the sister brought Viko to town, not to mention the mounting list of dead people, I've got to know. Were you aware that Scarlett was on this trail as well?"

Scarlett was Bain's wife, a reporter, and a good source to gather information. He hadn't had a chance to use her for any of this.

"What do you mean?" Boss looked toward Killian. He liked to be the first to know about everything, so this news didn't sit well with him.

"She got wind of the story about a week ago. Bain told me something about drug users going crazy in the emergency room, begging for help, holding their heads, banging them together. She's been tracing it all."

"Why wasn't I made aware of this?" Boss asked. "I want you to go to Bain and Scarlett's house, now. I need to talk to her."

Everything was going to shit. There was so much happening, one thing after the other, and he was struggling to keep up. Graciella distracted him and he wasn't going to pretend otherwise.

"What are you thinking?" Killian asked.

"I want to know what she knows."

"You think there's a chance she could know more than you?"

"If my memory serves me right, Scarlett has her means of getting what she wants. She managed to get under Bain's skin and that says a lot. Why wasn't I told of this before?" he asked.

"I believe Bain emailed you, or he may have left you a memo."

"Don't get fucking smart with me."

Killian had been born in an Irish whorehouse and his life had never been easy. Now he was happily married with kids. A family looked good on him.

"What's going on, Boss?" Killian asked. "This isn't like you and I don't like it."

Boss opened his mouth but went silent as his cell phone rang. He saw Maurice was calling. He answered. "I can't talk now, Maurice."

"Bain's in the hospital," Maurice said.

"What the fuck do you mean?" This wasn't good. This wasn't the kind of news he wanted to hear.

"Scarlett called the office. She needs you. Something's going on. She said she made a mistake and now she's terrified."

"We'll be there. Give me the address." In a large city, there were several major hospitals.

"What's going on?" Killian asked the moment he hung up.

"Bain's in the hospital and Scarlett needs help." He patted his knee, quickly putting the pieces together. "Bain took the drugs."

"What? That's not fucking possible. How could he have taken the drugs? The guy won't even take a painkiller. No, man, you've got that wrong."

"Something was bothering him this morning. He was … different today in the office. Sick. Fuck!" He slammed his fist against the front of the car. He'd gotten into this habit and with how strong he was, there were a few times he'd deployed the airbag. He had them all removed from the passenger side of the cars. He hated being hit in the face with it.

He gave Killian the address for the hospital.

Ignoring all the questions, as he didn't have any answers, he arrived at the hospital to find Scarlett in the waiting room. Her face was blanched and it was evident she'd been crying.

"Tell me what the fuck you know," Boss said.

"They're coming in disguised as mints," she said. "I was given this by a contact. It was completely sealed." She handed him the bag. "I think Bain took one, thinking they were mine." Tears were in her eyes. "What have I done? I let them out. I'm a fucking idiot. I think I just killed my husband."

Killing Scarlett wouldn't be good. Although tempting.

Of all his men, Bain had been handed the worst deck of cards when it came to childhoods. He felt for the man, fought hard to get him to work at Killer of Kings. He'd changed his life around … for what? To die in a hospital bed from tainted drugs?

He wanted to scream at Scarlett, tell her how stupid she was. Everything he'd discovered about these drugs, none of it was good.

He looked at Bain's wife. "Do you know the timeline?" he asked.

"No. What people don't know is how long from ingesting it that it takes effect." She sniffled.

"Bain didn't know you were working on this?"

"No. He's been so busy with his latest mission, I just worked on my own. This was new and every time we were together, I didn't want to talk work."

"You shouldn't have left them out in the open. You're a fucking idiot." And that was all he was going to say on the matter. If Bain died, he was going to have to make a choice, kill Scarlett, or make her live with the guilt of fucking up.

****

Graciella wasn't going to kill Boss.

Viko's offer, although tempting, wasn't going to work. He knew it and so did she. Boss was a good man.

A horrible, arrogant asshole, but he mostly did good work. He rarely took cases that meant the bad man won.

He killed bad men.

The men like the ones who'd taken her when she was a child, who made her suffer just because she was female. She hated men of all kinds, but Boss gave her hope. In her line of work, she'd seen the dark side in most.

Killing him wouldn't do the world good. It would allow the bad guys to flourish. In the underground, there needed to be checks and balances. The sharks couldn't be allowed to outnumber the fish.

Which was why walking into the hospital, she wore a pair of jeans and a floral shirt. Her hair was tied back, no makeup to speak of. This was not the façade she presented to the world. She'd heard what happened to Bain. One of Boss's men were in the hospital, and he needed her right now.

Xavier didn't even notice her as she stepped up to him.

"Hey," she said, looking at her brother.

He frowned at her and then his eyes went wide. "Graciella?"

She nodded.

He pulled her in his arms.

At first, she tensed up, ready to punch him, to keep some distance, but instead, she wrapped her arms around him. It was strange, for a long time, she had forgotten what it was like to have her brother's love, his protection, but it came to her fast and quick. She kept her eyes closed and relished the moment. She didn't know when she'd get another one, or if it would even be possible.

"I've got you," he said.

"I should be holding you."

"I didn't get to hold you enough," he said.

The reality. They'd been ripped apart from each other far too soon.

She pulled away. "Where is he?"

"In Bain's room. As usual, Boss took over. He's now in a private room and only the best doctors can see him."

"Can I go to him?"

"Did you know Bain?"

"No. I meant Boss. He's going to want to see me."

Xavier nodded. "A couple of the guys are there. So is Bain's wife."

She didn't say or do anything, merely followed. Hospitals were the worst of places. She'd been taken to hospitals after a client had beaten her up—before she knew how to take care of herself. People had been paid off to not ask too many questions. She'd had no one.

Walking into Bain's room, she saw some of the Killer of Kings men, and wow, they all look pissed. With them in the room, she felt small. She wasn't a tall woman, and at that moment, she couldn't believe she actually rivaled them with her kills and her ability to strike.

Boss looked at her. "Are you going to kill me?"

"No."

"Really? You're not going to take the job? It promises a big payday. I understand you have a shitload of debt."

"You and I both know Viko did it on purpose. He doesn't want me to pay off my debt."

"Debt, what debt?" Xavier asked.

"It's nothing." She kept her gaze on Boss. It wasn't a shock to her that he already knew about what Viko had asked. There was no way she was going to underestimate him again. "What do you know?"

"First of all, you're going to have to tell us what you know about this," Boss said, getting to his feet. "I'm not playing games, not anymore. That's my man in here."

She moved toward the door and closed it. "I only know so much but what you've got to understand is this drug has changed. What I originally had planned for it, it has changed."

"Then tell me what little you do fucking know because right now, we're on a clock. He's not going to die, do you understand me?"

There was no mistaking the edge to his voice. Boss was holding on by a thread and if she wasn't careful, he was going to take it out on her.

"How did he get it?" she asked.

The only other woman in the room stood up and held out a plastic bag. Taking it from her, Graciella frowned. "I've never seen it like this. They're masking the original product." She rolled the clear bag of mints over in her hand. They weren't a recognizable brand, nor did they appear like any mints she'd ever seen.

"How did it come to you?" Boss asked.

"As raw drugs. They weren't disguised like this when we started, but we can use this for tracing."

"Wait a minute," Xavier said. "You created this product?"

Graciella tensed as each of the Killer of Kings turned toward her. She looked at each of their faces. There was no mistaking the unspoken accusation, and they all wanted her dead.

"I did this to avenge my childhood." She glared at each of them. "You have to understand, the men I planned to kill using this, it was only supposed to be for them. I had complete control until it was snatched away

71

from me. I was a child when these men passed me around, raped me, beat me. I was the entertainment when they got drunk. I was going to make sure they suffered. I'd been well-trained, but I couldn't take them all out, so I used the drugs. I used their greatest asset against them. I'm not ashamed of what I did. What I am ashamed of is believing I could wipe its existence from the face of the fucking earth. That was my one and only mistake."

Tears were in Xavier's eyes. Scarlett sobbed. The men didn't look ready to kill her. Not anymore.

"Don't pity me," she said. "What your friend is going to go through isn't pretty, and we don't have a lot of time. This took twenty-four hours, seventy-two at the most, but I don't know the full compounds, and the last time I checked, these were not reversible. All of the cases I've read about, the men and women couldn't be saved."

"I've got the doctor running a full tox screen," Boss said.

"We need the scientist. Only he would know how to treat it."

"There's no guarantee of that though, is there?" Scarlett asked, her voice shaking. "This was designed to kill. You said so yourself. Why create an antidote?"

Graciella looked at Boss. "Because if this is the same scientist I used, he once told me that no one would create something where there was a risk of it coming back and biting them. For every dosage, there would be an antidote. In fact, we argued because he took longer than I wanted. He wouldn't give me the drugs until he was sure he had an antidote. I don't have any. I had no intention of taking the stuff, so I didn't bother to get some. If I did, I'd have given it to you."

"How can we trust you?" Killian asked. "All you have done is cause us trouble. We're cleaning up your mess."

"You think I'm not trying to clean this up? Why do you think I've moved as much as I have? Why I happen to appear when the cases of the crazed druggies are rife? I'm following it. I'm trying to trace it, and this is all I've got." She held up the mints. "This is the biggest clue."

Her hands shook.

"We need to talk," Boss said. He put a hand to her back and started to walk her out of the room but Xavier stood in front of the door.

The pain in her brother's eyes was clear to see. This was torture to her. He was the only family she had left. It was one of the many reasons why she tried to ignore him. Seeing him now, it was hard to stay cool and aloof.

"I hope one day you can forgive me," he said.

"Xavier," she said.

"Now is not the time," Boss interrupted and nudged her forward.

"There's nothing to be forgiven for," she said.

Opening the door, she let Boss take the lead, guiding her to where he wanted her.

Boss came to a stop at an office. They stepped inside and she looked around. There were no cameras and there were several machines where doctors used x-rays.

Hands on her hips, she looked at him. "I didn't want this to happen. I hope you believe that. I'm not a monster."

"Why won't you kill me?" he asked.

"Really, you want to know that?"

"I don't need to know it today, but it's a question you're going to have to answer. For now, tell me all that you know about Viko."

"You think he's distributing the drug?" she asked.

"I know Viko and he's the kind of guy who would mask drugs as something else. It helps get them through shipping into the country and doesn't require backyard dealings."

"Viko didn't do this."

"You sound confident. How do you know?"

She took a deep breath. "Because … the debt to him, it goes deeper than his protection of me."

"What do you mean?"

She didn't want to reveal another man's business. She took a deep breath. The only way to finally combat these drugs was to work together. "Viko's tracing the drugs as well. He has been for a couple of years. What you don't know is he once had a daughter. I won't get into the details, but she had a boyfriend and … well, he got her into drugs. These things got to her, and she died. Viko, for all of his faults, is on your side. He wants the scientists and the people behind them."

Chapter Seven

Boss didn't have time to play around. Not with Bain's life in the balance. The possibility of losing him was indigestible—but his man was strong, and if anyone could survive this, it would be Bain.

He lay on his stomach on the roof of the seven-story building. Business never stopped at Killer of Kings. He'd wanted to take his time with this contract, savor it. But at this point, he just needed it done. The heat was getting to him, but he didn't flinch. He was a statue, his eyes on the doorway of the building across the busy street. Maurice had tracked his movements, and Mr. Black always worked out at this gym, same time, same day. Never smart for a man working on the shady side of the law to have a predictable schedule.

As soon as he had Tyson Black in his sights, he pulled the trigger. It only took one shot. Boss never missed.

Immediately, he rolled into a sitting position and packed up his sniper rifle. Clean and quick. There was only one more to take care of—Edward Seer. He'd wanted to do this himself, but finding the scientist was now his top priority.

He pulled out his cell as he jogged down the staircase to the street below. "Chains, I have a find and eliminate I need you to handle. The client's family was threatened."

"Send me the info. I'll get it done."

"Wait for my secure message. Check for loose ends. Make sure no one hurts the wife or kid."

"You know it."

Boss slipped his phone back into his pocket. Chains didn't like men hurting women, so he was the right man for the job. He trusted all his hitmen to efficiently handle their contracts, which was why he rarely took any jobs himself. Maybe he'd stick to overseeing.

He carefully put his rifle case in his trunk and got behind the driver's seat of his car. He called Adam as he started up the engine. "News?"

"I'm working on something right now, Boss. It's big. I've been coordinating with Maurice and we've tracked these mints to a factory out of state. Shipments came in by water in containers. The trail leads to an island in the Caribbean. You'll find your scientist there."

"Soaking up the sun, enjoying the spoils of the suffering he's caused." Boss gripped the steering wheel with his right hand, squeezing so hard his knuckles turned white. "Tell Maurice I want a flight—tickets for me, Graciella, Killian, and Xavier. Tonight. Get me as much intel as you can—names, addresses, everything."

"Yes, Boss. I'll get it handled."

In his world, money and power talked. Now that he had a major lead, that scientist was as good as dead. Once he had his hands on the antidote, he'd give it to Adam to synthesize. The cycle of death from Graciella's revenge would end.

He could be her hero.

As he drove home, he messaged his men so they could say their goodbyes to their families. Then he called Widow Maker.

"What do you want now?" she answered.

He chuckled. "I've found your scientist. Thought you'd want to know."

There was silence on the other end of the line.

"Unless you'd rather I keep information to myself," he said.

"No, I want to be in the loop. Are you sure about this? It's not a hunch?"

"I wouldn't gamble with Bain's life. We tracked the drug mints Scarlett had right to the source country. Now it's just a game of cat and mouse," he said.

"Give me what you have. I can handle anything."

He smiled to himself. Boss loved her spunk and defiance. She'd never bend over for anyone and he liked that about her. "Of that, I'm certain. I'll call you when I have more details."

She growled and hung up the phone.

He laughed out loud. She drove him crazy and was sexy as fuck. She was also his greatest weakness. He always kept track of his killers' women. Since he'd been hung up on Graciella, he'd been slacking in all areas. If it hadn't been for his obsession, he would have caught wind of Scarlett's activity long before Bain got poisoned.

Would have, could have wouldn't help him now. It was time to make things right for everyone. Once the drug ordeal was over, what would happen to Graciella's debt to Viko? She'd have no reason to team up with him once her problem was gone. Only the debt would remain.

Boss would pay for her freedom if he had to.

He pulled into his underground parking area, the doors automatically closing behind his car. He put his jacket on the hook and headed upstairs. There wasn't much time to get ready for a trip abroad. Boss scrubbed his hands over his face and looked in the hall mirror. He was too old for this shit.

The front doorbell chimed, echoing in the massive foyer. His mansion had too many empty rooms. It wasn't until now that he realized how sterile his home was. Graciella was right. He was just as lonely as her.

He opened the front door, El Diablo and Killian pushed through the doorway like two toddlers needing to be first.

"Dominican Republic?" asked Xavier.

"How long will we be gone?" asked Killian.

Boss took a deep breath. "I'm going to take a shower, pack a bag, then we're all heading to the airport so we can save Bain."

"You found what we need?" asked Killian.

Boss nodded.

"What about firepower?" asked Xavier.

"Everything's already being arranged as we speak. We'll pick up our guns as soon as we're off the airplane. I have contacts on the island."

"There were five more local deaths today," said Killian as he dropped down in one of the armchairs.

Boss groaned. "You're not fucking helping. We're leaving in an hour. Make sure you're both ready. Graciella's on her way."

"Graciella? Why does she need to come?" asked Xavier.

Boss chuckled as he walked up the winding staircase. "Funny, I know she'd say the same thing about you. Your sister's not a little girl, Xavier. She can handle herself."

He didn't wait to hear more complaints.

Boss headed to his bedroom, stripped down, and stepped into his custom walk-in shower. He turned on the rainfall head and stood beneath the cooling water.

He thought of Graciella, her gorgeous body under him on the bed. She was fucking perfect. Luscious curves, evil eyes, and the scars inside and out only attracted him more. She was complicated and lethal. He'd often had female assassins work for him. They were employees, nothing more. Graciella was something else.

The door to his bathroom burst open. Boss leaned over and grabbed a towel, wrapping it securely around his waist.

"What the fuck?"

He had two of his hitmen downstairs. How did anyone manage to get upstairs?

Graciella stood there in the middle of the large room wearing all black leather, her dark hair brushed smooth as glass over her back and shoulders. Her hands were perched on her hips as she stared directly at him.

"Did you kill my men?"

She tilted her head, eyes narrowed. "They didn't try to stop me."

"What's the problem here?" He stepped out of the shower and grabbed a hand towel to pat dry his face.

"You're the problem," she snapped. "Who do you think you are, anyway? You think you can toy with me because you're the killer of kings?"

He ignored her ranting, walking to the wall of counters. Boss ran both hands through his damp hair, looking at her through the reflection in the mirror.

"I'm talking to you!" She stormed over to him, her heels clicking on the marble. "You didn't think I should be involved in killing the scientist? I'm the one he screwed over. I'm the one who's had to live with this on my conscience."

Her emotion and vitriol were palpable. He loved her like this. So much fucking passion.

Boss grabbed his shaving cream container and began to spread some foam under his chin. "Are you done?"

"Bastard!" She had a blade tight to his throat the next second. "You thought you could fly off in the night and I'd be none the wiser?"

"Don't start something unless you plan to follow through," he warned.

"Do you know how many men I've killed for less?"

Boss hadn't moved, the sharp edge of the blade nicking his skin. "Do you realize how many women I've turned down since that night in the restaurant?"

She scoffed. "I don't care about your whores. What does that have to do with anything?"

In a few quick moves, he knocked the blade from her hand, the metal tinking into the sink, then twisted her body around so she was trapped between the counter and his much larger frame. "Because I can't get you off my mind."

"You'll get over it."

She wriggled, but he forced her to stay in place.

"You feel nothing at all? Are you really that cold, Graciella?" he asked. "You still haven't answered me—why didn't you kill me?"

"I should have." She glared daggers at him then tried to knee him in the crotch. He blocked her move, securing her wrists. She twirled and ducked, freeing herself, then she kicked him in the side. He groaned and ground his teeth together.

Restraining himself was becoming increasingly difficult.

****

Graciella was pissed off.

Boss had called to tell her he'd found the scientist. In a way, they were all a team with the same goal. It felt good, and they were making progress together. Then he pulled this bullshit. He was flying out with Killian and Xavier to kill the scientist who'd fucked up years of her life. People had died because of those drugs, and that was all on her, not Boss.

She was tired of being treated like a second-rate killer because she was a woman. Graciella had a lot to prove, but she thought Boss was better than that. She was wrong.

Boss glared at her after she kicked him for the second time. She knew she was playing with fire, but she couldn't stop herself.

"You're even taking Xavier."

"Your brother will blend well in the Dominican Republic. He speaks the language and can get us good intel once we're on the ground."

"In case you haven't noticed, I have the same qualifications. But I'm of no importance to you, am I?"

Her breathing was rapid, her chest rising and falling in deep waves.

"If any other person, man or woman, had come in here without permission, they'd be dead," he said.

"Not me?"

"You like to test me, don't you?"

"I like to be included and not constantly out of the loop. Did you think I'd slow you down? Put your man in the hospital at risk?"

She attempted to strike him, but he snatched her wrist so fast she gasped. He wasn't so gentle this time. Boss had her stomach down over the counter. His bathroom was nearly as big as her condo, floor-to-ceiling marble, the epitome of luxury. Maybe she was in way over her head testing the king.

Graciella felt the hard ridge of his cock against her ass. He secured both her wrists above her head and collected her hair to one side with the other. He leaned over and kissed her temple. She squirmed, but he only squeezed her wrists tighter in warning. Graciella was only alive right now because he'd had mercy on her for some reason.

"Your temper is your weakness, beauty," he whispered in her ear.

He released her wrists, and she immediately twisted around. Boss grabbed her waist and hoisted her up on the counter, using a thigh to separate her legs.

She swallowed hard. Boss wasn't a meek man. His frame was big and hard with muscle. He was always in control, even when she pushed him too far. She could feel the heat of his skin, smell the musky scent of his shaving cream, and savored his strength as he grabbed her ass and pulled her to the edge of the counter.

"Take what you want. That's what you do, isn't it?"

"Watch it. Think twice before you speak to me." He stood there for another few seconds, staring her down, then he stepped away and carried on as if she wasn't there. "Top drawer," he said.

She slipped down and opened the first drawer, keeping him in her sights at all times. He was only shaving in front of a sink, no sense of fear or urgency even though she'd attacked him numerous times.

Graciella pulled out the contents of the envelope. They were plane tickets with her name on them. First class to the Dominican Republic.

She was shocked into silence.

"I don't understand. If you had these the whole time … why didn't you say anything?"

"That wouldn't be any fun."

Her temper boiled up once again. She waved the envelope next to him. "You're too much, do you know that?"

He leaned over the splashed his face with water, patted his skin dry, then added after-shave. His body still glistened from his shower, every defined muscle moving as he cleaned up by the counter.

"Considering this was all your doing, you're lucky I'm involving you at all."

She wanted to tell him off, but he was right. Her mistake had even crossed borders. And she knew he was worried sick about Bain.

Graciella wanted to kick herself. This wasn't what she was expecting. "I'm sorry," she said.

"For what? Trying to slit my throat?"

"For not checking with you first…"

Boss narrowed his eyes. He slipped on his clean boxers under the towel, not giving her a glimpse, then hung up the towel on the bar. His movements were slow, and she could feel his disapproval even though she hadn't said anything yet.

"Go on," he said.

She took a deep breath. "I called Viko. Told him about the island, your tickets, and the scientist."

He chewed on his lower lip. It would be sexy as hell if she wasn't certain he wanted to kill her just then. "Who called you?"

Graciella shrugged.

"Was it El Diablo? Fucking tell me right now."

"No! I swear it wasn't him," she said. Boss looked like he wanted to assassinate her brother, murder in his eyes. But it wasn't Xavier.

He stalked closed, caging her in. "Now."

"Me."

One eyebrow raised in question, then he exhaled. "You tagged me. When? Where?"

"No, I tapped Xavier's phone. Men are all the same," she said. "So easy to manipulate."

He chuckled, a deep masculine sound that affected her way too much.

"That's where you're wrong, sweetheart. The only one who manages to fuck with my head is you." He kept coming closer. She didn't try to stop him.

Boss was a breath away. He leaned down to her level, running his lips along her cheek, slowly, so close to her lips. He inhaled, exhaling on a faint growl. She wanted to touch him, to grab on to those strong shoulders.

She closed her eyes.

"Why didn't you kill me?" he whispered in her ear.

When she didn't answer, he cupped his big hand under her pussy. The pressure was intense when she was already strung high with her attraction for Boss. She dropped her weight just enough so she could feel more. Her lips parted slightly, and he moved in fast, kissing her with enough passion to steal all her thoughts.

Her natural defenses vanished. Her anger fizzled away.

If she was his weakness, he was hers just as much.

Should she give in to her desires? God knew how much she wanted Boss. Wanted him to ride her. He wasn't an evil man. Would it be so bad to allow herself to experience the pleasure he could give her? He prided himself at being the best at everything.

She wasn't sure what she wanted out of Boss.

Did she want the whole fairy tale? She'd never really thought about it. Was that even possible for people as broken as them?

No, if she let down the guards around her heart, she'd regret it.

She was the conquest right now. Once Boss claimed her, she'd be discarded like all the others. That, she couldn't handle. It was safer for her to call the shots.

"Do you like that?" The way he moved his hands, one on her crotch, the other behind her neck was addicting. He knew exactly how to handle her body to make her spineless in his arms.

She swallowed hard, not willing to give him the satisfaction. Inside, she was screaming, *yes, yes, yes!*

He began teasing the shell of her ear with his tongue. "You tell me when you're ready, baby girl. I promise you won't regret it." He moved his hands, cupping her ass with both of them, pulling her against his impressive cock. He never stopped kissing her—her jaw, her neck, then back to her lips. This time, she draped her arms around him, their kiss deepening. She panted and mewled, rubbing her body against him, not to seduce, but because she needed more of him.

She was close to begging, her entire body craving everything Boss.

"It's a long flight. How about you take a quick shower?" He unzipped the front of her leather corset, taking his time, revealing her satin bra. He trailed a finger down the center of her cleavage and she shivered involuntarily. "Such a beautiful body. I want it to be mine."

Graciella looked down. What was he talking about? There were so many old cigarette burns on her breasts. All her confidence was a façade.

He peeled the cup of one bra down, giving her time to protest—she didn't. Her nipple was pebbled and aching for attention. She held her breath as he went down on her, covering her breast with his hot mouth. The strength in her legs gave out, so he hoisted her up. She wrapped herself around him as he carried her back to the counter. Why wasn't he continuing what he started? She felt like she'd spontaneously combust at any second.

"I want to fuck you so bad right now," he said. Instead of bringing her to his bed as she hoped he would, he combed both hands into her hair, securing her head. That fire was back in his eyes. "But business first. What did you tell Viko?"

Disappointment assaulted her.

She exhaled and panted for breath. There was no

disguising her need.

"He's taking the next flight to the Dominican. He wants to ensure the hit is done. He needs to satisfy his own demons."

"Next time, keep him out of it. Do you understand? The only reason he allows you to live is out of pity. If you think otherwise, you're living a pipe dream."

"I'm not in love with Viko."

She wasn't.

He was a means to get what she needed, and there were many days she regretted asking for his help. Being indebted to anyone was the last thing she wanted in her life.

"I never said you were. But I don't want you disillusioned by him."

"What about you, Boss? Should I trust you with my body? With my heart?"

There were heavy footsteps coming up the stairs, stealing the moment.

Boss frowned then zipped up her shirt for her. "Your brother is really starting to piss me off."

Chapter Eight

"I'm sorry," Graciella said a couple of hours later, not for the first time. She even clenched her teeth when she said it. No matter how she spoke, she always seemed to struggle with those two simple words. Now, he just found it funny to actually listen to her struggle.

It was cute.

While the rest of his men had gotten a hotel room, Graciella included, she'd snuck into his.

Standing at the bar in his hotel room, Boss stared at his problem. He took a cleansing breath and dropped two ice cubes into a glass with a clink. He should have known to quickly check his flight to see if there was a problem the moment he got wind of Viko knowing about the scientist. He was pissed.

This was *his* hit, *his* plan. His everything. He'd wanted to be the one to save her. To finally end the demons chasing her. She was a woman made of ice but there was a heart in there somewhere. It was killing her to know people were dying. People like Bain who might mistake the drugs for mints and take them.

It was so fucking stupid. When he did save Bain, he was going to put him through an intense course of "don't fucking take shit you don't recognize."

"Boss, come on," she said.

"What do you want from me?" he asked. "You called Viko. He decided to ground me, to take out my pilot, our flight, and to deal with this shit on his own. The last time I checked, the Circle of Monsters didn't have our finesse, so our scientist would get wind of not one, but two organizations after him. He's probably already fleeing the country. My element of surprise is fucked!"

"Boss, I'm sorry."

He advanced toward her. "You're used to being

on your own." She took a step back. "When you're in my world, you work as a team."

"Working as a team gets you dead."

"Xavier used to think that and now he's a team player. You should try it sometime."

"I'm not having this conversation with you." The wall stopped her leave. He slammed his hands at either side of her head. He knew they weren't evenly matched. The Widow Maker was good, but she wasn't him. Not even close. He was the best. He'd owned the title for many years, and he would continue to do so until someone put a bullet in his head.

"No, like always, you're going to piss me off and run away. That's your MO. It's what you do, always. All you *will* do. You know why? Because you're afraid."

"How dare you."

"How dare I? How fucking dare you," he said. "You come into my world. Turn it fucking upside down, and now the kill I can make to help you, you turn it over to a man who doesn't have my skill."

She paused. "What?"

"You heard me." He wasn't in the habit of repeating himself and he wasn't about to start now.

He was so close to offering her salvation. Damn it, he could taste it. This science guy, he had a reputation for dirty deals. Did Graciella even know that? Was she aware that there was a reason the son of bitch was willing to make her drugs?

Staring at her now, he wanted to hold her. To kiss her. To fuck her senseless. It was on her. He wouldn't touch her again, not until she begged him for it.

"This is all for Bain," she said.

"Not all of it. Capturing your scientist, getting the antidote from him, that will be saving Bain. Killing him is all for you. I hunted him for *you*."

"Why?"

"You know why."

"But, I'm not a nice person. I'm really not." She cleared her throat and he cupped her face.

"Look at me, Graciella."

She tilted her head back but her eyes were closed. Always rebelling.

He pressed a kiss to each of her eyelids. As much as he was pissed off, he wasn't going to hurt her. He couldn't. Boss pulled away and was surprised to see tears.

"Why are you crying?"

"I can't help it."

Boss stepped away.

A couple of tears slowly traced down her cheeks but she gave no other sign of emotion.

"I don't know what's going on right now," he said.

"I … no one has ever done anything like that for me before. I'm not used to it." She licked her lips. "I've been on my own for so long."

"You're not on your own."

"All you want from me is to join you." She swiped at her cheeks as if the tears offended her. "This is so stupid."

"You think that's all I care about?" he asked.

"Isn't it? You're not trying to grow your little clique?"

He scoffed. "We're not in high school. Yes, I want you as part of Killer of Kings, but not just because you're a good assassin." He had to touch her. Running his thumb across her bottom lip, he wanted to taste her. Instead, he stared into her eyes, trying to keep his wits about him. "I want to keep an eye on you, Graciella. I don't know what it is you've done to me, but I can't help but want to take care of you."

"I don't need a babysitter."

He laughed. "I don't think of you as a child. Believe me, I don't." He pressed his rock-hard cock against her. "Feel that. Feel me. This is what you do to me. I can't seem to control myself around you and it fucking does my head in. I'm a man of self-control."

She took him by surprise as she wrapped her arms around his neck and slammed her lips against his. He tasted the saltiness of her tears. He wrapped his arms around her, one going to her ass, lifting her up, and resting her against the wall.

Her legs went around his waist and he was nestled right against her core. She felt so fucking good.

She traced her tongue across his lips and he opened up, deepening the kiss. This woman was running riot with his emotions. One moment he was pissed and wanted to throttle her, the next, he couldn't get enough of her and wanted nothing more than to fuck her.

The kiss slowly eased, the passion not dying but Graciella pulling away. She released his waist, putting her legs back to the ground.

"I've never had a man put my needs first," she said. Her hand touched his lips. "I enjoy kissing you. I think you're the first man in my entire life that I've kissed and really enjoyed it."

"Graciella?"

"I told Viko because I want him to be in your debt. I don't want him to put your head up for bounty and if you piss him off, he will do it." She licked her lips and stepped back. "I don't … I'm not used to having people care. I know my brother does and I … I love him too, but it's not the same." She took a deep breath. "I hope one day you can understand, and I'm sorry. If Viko gets the scientist, he did promise he'd give you the antidote."

"You shouldn't have done it."

"I know, but for your safety, I'd do it again." She walked away and headed to the door.

He wanted to stop her but knew that kiss alone was more than she'd been willing to give at some point. Beneath all the confidence was a broken soul. This was her attempt to reach out.

She opened the door.

"Thank you," he said.

She lifted her head and nodded.

"Let's hope you didn't fuck up and kill Bain in the process."

He watched her take a deep breath. "I ... I wouldn't have done it if I didn't believe in him, Boss. I know he's an asshole and he does things differently, but he's a good man. To a certain extent."

Boss watched her as she closed the door.

When he got his hands on Viko, that fucker was going to die.

Just as he was about to finish dressing, another knock came at his door. He wasn't in the mood for company. He was already on a clock, and right now, he was behind schedule. His arms dealer was calling him within the hour to make new arrangements. There was a lot to get done before they stormed the warehouse.

Bain's life hung in the balance.

"Come in," he said.

Xavier entered.

"What now?" he asked.

"I saw my sister leave."

"And if you have an issue, go and see her."

"I know something's going on between the two of you."

Boss laughed, but it wasn't a happy sound.

"And? What do you want me to do? I'm your

boss and the last time I checked, your sister was of age. If she didn't want anything to happen, she could end my fucking life." He was done playing nice.

"Boss, I get that she can handle herself. I've only just got her back and I'm worried."

"You really think I'm going to be the one to drive her away?" Boss asked.

"It's what I'm worried about."

"Look, Xavier, I get it. You're worried about her, but right now, Bain's in the hospital dying. My guys are doing everything they can to try and prolong his life. What happens between Graciella and me is our business. I'm not going to confer with you, but what I will tell you is everything I do with her, I will never hurt her. You have my word."

"The thing is, Boss, you use people."

"And you think the Widow Maker doesn't?" he asked. He was fast losing patience. All he wanted to do was have a drink and reorganize his plan. None of that was working for him right now.

"She's more than that," Xavier said.

"I know. Now get the fuck out of my room so I can clean up her mess and whatever fuckup Viko has made." He went to his door, opened it, determined to clean everything so everyone fucking lived.

Being the head of Killer of Kings was starting to make him feel more and more like a parent of spoiled little brats.

****

Graciella had hoped Viko wouldn't let his emotions get the better of him, but as they arrived at the location Boss had, it looked like that was very much not the case.

Not only was there no sign of the scientist, but Viko was also there with a mostly empty bottle of whiskey, and a gun, and it was aimed at all of them.

"I should have known you'd be on their side," Viko said.

It was rare for Viko to lose control.

She kept her gaze on him. His men stood behind him, hand on their guns, ready to shoot.

"I take it you didn't make your fucking arrival confidential?" Boss asked, stepping away from them and glancing around the factory. There were a few packets on the floor, but it looked like it had been packed up fast.

The operation wasn't as big as she imagined it would be. The factory itself was small compared to most.

Viko burst out laughing, the sound of a crazed man.

The journey to the Dominican had been uncomfortable. None of the Killer of Kings wanted to talk to her. Even Boss had focused on his laptop, not giving her a single glance.

She should be pissed off.

Instead, she just stared out of the window and chanted to herself how safe it was to be on the airplane. She hated flying.

Hated it, despised it, often had nightmares of the plane going down into waters and being swallowed whole by a giant octopus, or eaten by piranhas. She very much preferred driving. Something to stay on the ground. Nice firm ground.

"Go ahead, Boss, shoot me. You and your boys want to do it. Go ahead," Viko said. "What about you, Graciella? Want to shoot me?"

"Not today."

He snorted and lifted his gun. It was pointed at her forehead.

She looked at him. There an especially sore spot within her when it came to drunks. Men used alcohol as an excuse for their vile behavior. There was no fear inside her, only acceptance.

"I should kill you," he said.

Graciella didn't need to look back to know the Killer of Kings were tensed and poised. She didn't reach for her gun. She knew Viko, not intimately, but enough to know he wasn't going to shoot her.

"Go ahead."

"You told me that son of a bitch was here!"

"He was here," Boss said. He had his gun out. "You kill her and that's it, it's over."

"We'll have a good old-fashioned shootout. You think you'll make it out alive, Boss? You're good. Maybe you're better than me, but I always have a plan. I have a lot of fucking plans in place and if you kill me, I'll make sure you don't get to sleep without someone breathing down your neck. I wonder how the Killer leader would be after weeks of no sleep. That calm exterior would certainly crumble."

"Viko, we will find him," she said.

His hand hadn't wavered.

"We will."

His jaw clenched. She saw the man slowly falling apart. "You know it was a thing of beauty. Your plan. Killing your enemies with their own product. I never had such vision. Sure, I've killed a lot of people but yours, yours was poetry. They got to see you and know what you'd done. You got your perfect revenge."

"I know."

"I never… It was supposed to fucking end there."

"I know. I didn't anticipate what happened," she said.

"I should have known. She would—" Viko didn't finish. Still, his hand didn't shake. She took a step toward him.

This was the first time in all the years she'd known Viko that she'd seen any kind of real emotion. He'd always been stone cold. Alcohol had a way of pulling demons to the surface.

"She'd still be alive," she finished for him.

"Graciella?" Xavier said.

She ignored her brother's warning or Boss's cleared throat. Going to one knee, she did something she never thought she would do, she hugged Viko. He didn't touch her. The gun was still trained in the air.

"You!" He growled the word.

She held him a little tighter.

Boss nor Xavier understood. Yes, she hated Viko with a passion, was indebted to him, but in a weird kind of way, he was also her friend. They'd been through a lot together.

"I killed her," he said.

"You didn't."

"It's my job to save her. My job!" His gun dropped as did the bottle and his arms went limp. The scent of expensive whiskey wafted up as it spilled across the concrete floor.

"I know," Graciella said.

She'd never met Viko's daughter. That was how protective he was of her, but she'd gotten glimpses of his little princess. The only person close to his heart. There had been rumors he had a wife at one point, or a whore. The information about him was as vague as Boss's.

"What is going on right now?" Killian asked.

"I don't know," Xavier said.

Silence rang out.

Time passed.

She didn't know how much time but she sensed the impatience of the men, and it was increasing with every passing minute.

Bain would die.

Viko pulled away and stood up. There were no tears. Of course, there weren't. He looked away.

"I don't have time for this shit," Boss said. "I get it, you lost someone important to you. You think the Circle of Monsters can handle this shit? You guys are known for creating an entrance. What this needed was fucking delicacy, which you don't have."

Viko glared at him.

"I heard about Bain," Viko said. "My daughter, she was … she was young when she was given the drugs. I've been hunting this son of a bitch for some time." He put his hands on his hips.

"Well, maybe it's time for you to back away and not to do any of this shit anymore," he said. "You're clearly too close to it all."

"Do not tell me what I can and cannot do," he said. "I'm not in the mood to listen. Not now." Viko ran a hand down his face. "Let's go."

Graciella watched, expecting Boss to complain, but he didn't. They all stood by and watched as Viko and his men left the factory.

She turned toward Boss, who was staring at her.

"Congratulations," he said. He stepped up close to her and she was shocked as he put a set of handcuffs on her wrists.

"What the fuck are you doing?" She tugged at her wrists.

"I've got one hell of a guy and he was able to put a trace on some of the technology they were using. He's waiting for it to stop moving and the moment it does, we're going to follow. For now, it's about three hours from this location, heading east. We're going to follow it. Xavier, take her phone."

Before she had a chance to stop her brother, her

cell phone was taken.

"Hey!" she yelled, glaring at her brother, pissed.

The cuffs couldn't keep her for long.

"Killian, the hair."

The clips and pins were removed from her hair.

Piece by piece, it was all removed. Even her earrings. She stood in only her clothes, which didn't have any metal she could use to remove the cuffs.

"The last time you were left alone, you screwed this up. I'm not going to give you a chance again."

"And you really think this is the way to do it?" she asked, glaring at him.

"I think it's the best way of keeping you close, yes. You want to tag me, that's fine, but I've got my own methods for keeping you close. This way, you're going to know every single little detail as I do, and you're not going to get a chance to squeal."

How had he known she'd put a tracker on him? She was an idiot to think she could outsmart Boss.

"Xavier, seriously, you can't let this happen."

"Sorry, Graciella, but you only seem to want to use me when it will appeal to you. Bain's a friend. I want to save him, and you're putting the whole operation at risk. None of us can let that happen."

"I didn't mean to." That was the truth.

"But you did," Boss said. "Let's go." He was already heading out of the factory, Xavier and Killian hot on his tail. She was annoyed with herself for screwing up. She should have known deep down Viko couldn't handle this. He was too emotionally involved.

Her emotions were in check. Even Boss, his emotions were also part of all of this.

She tried to think. The science guy had been her biggest mistake.

She had to fix this somehow, but she couldn't

think of how best to do it, and it pissed her off.

"Do we know who he's working for yet?" Graciella called out.

Boss didn't say anything.

"Oh, for goodness sake, just talk to me. I've got no cell phone, and I need to think. We know where the scientist is, and how he's getting the drugs across the border, but this guy wouldn't have this much cash or the resources for a scale this big. Whoever this is, he's got backing. Who the fuck is it?" she asked.

Boss turned to look at her.

"You don't know, do you?" she asked.

"So far, we know the scientist has had a great deal of funds transferred into his account. Maurice is working through the codes and firewalls to trace it. Each account and avenue has led to a dead end. We know he's being funded and with a scale like that, there have to be guards as well." Boss tapped his leg then pulled out his cell phone. "Maurice, hack into the security footage. Not at the factory, their cameras are minimal and fake. No, I want you to check across the street."

He hung up his cell phone.

"Why across the street?" she asked.

"There's a café across the street, the only one within the area. I figure everyone gets hungry, including our scientist, and if he's working with someone, he needs to be protected. If Maurice can get the information we need, we can find who he's working for. We can remove this chain of evil once and for all."

Chapter Nine

"You're not actually leaving her here alone, are you?" asked El Diablo. They were all getting into the SUV outside the warehouse. "This place is a shithole."

"Get in the fucking car," said Boss.

They drove down the rough roadway, the vehicle jostling and jolting. It would be a long three hours. They weren't in his city anymore. Far from home. These towns were overcrowded, poverty-stricken, and crime ran rampant. El Diablo worried about his sister being left alone in a foreign town with no phone or money. Boss knew better.

He never underestimated Widow Maker. And when they crossed paths again, she'd be fucking pissed—he couldn't wait.

Viko's car drove close behind theirs. It was bad enough he'd fucked up their surprise arrival, so Boss wouldn't let him screw up their second chance to get the antidote from the scientist.

"Any update from Maurice?" asked Boss.

Killian got on his cell in the back seat.

Their driver, Rocco, worked for Killer of Kings, and he was following the initial lead. "The locals can smell a foreigner from a mile away," he said. "Don't be surprised if they try to jack us."

Boss scoffed. "Just keep driving."

About twenty minutes later, he got a call from Maurice.

"You were right about the cameras across the street. I captured the scientist with the same man three times in the past week. It loops after that. I've run his profile and got a hit."

"Anyone we know?" asked Boss.

"Inside politics, I'm afraid. Your friend Viko

should watch his back."

"What now?"

"Manuel Adrino Viola. He's worked within the Circle of Monsters for a few years. Errand boy. Looks like he may be trying to make a play for Viko's place in the circle."

"By distributing these tainted drugs?"

"That's as much as I have right now, Boss."

"Send me everything you have to my secure email. Find out who he's been talking to. Check his bank accounts."

That was one of the problems when you hired any lowlife criminal to do your dirty work. There was no loyalty. The Circle of Monsters was a band of rogue killers looking to get paid. They couldn't be compared to the Killer of Kings on their best day.

They arrived in the rural town over three hours later. Boss needed to take a piss. They all got out of the vehicles, doors slamming, the sound of crickets droning in the fields of tall grass. There wasn't much in the little rundown town, just a few dilapidated structures. It was completely off the grid, no signs of life. No people or cars. He didn't like it.

"You sure this is it?" Boss asked Rocco.

He pointed. "The signal is coming from one of those two buildings."

Viko came up alongside him. He reeked of alcohol but appeared to be somewhat sober. "Where is he? I want to be the one to kill him."

"Relax, will you? You're not fucking this one up. Keep back while I handle it. This entire shitshow is on you now," said Boss.

"He got scared off before we got on scene. There's no way to know when that happened."

Boss didn't have time to argue. "Who's Manuel

Viola to you?"

Viko narrowed his eyes. "A guy I use. Why?"

Boss chuckled. "The Circle of Fuckups. Your guy's trying to bury you in this mess. He's paying the scientist. Manuel wants your place in the circle."

Viko's expression changed, his features setting hard. "That's not possible. Where would he get the money to fund processing these drugs? He's nobody," said Viko.

"He could have gone into debt. How the fuck should I know?"

Like Graciella had mentioned, this scale of this project needed cash.

"If it's true, he'll live to regret the day he crossed me." He walked back to where his four men were standing. Boss ignored them, keeping on task.

"Xavier, Killian … weapons."

"We're ready, Boss."

"Remember, our number one priority is the antidote. We can clean up shit later. Think about Bain."

Killian nodded. "Hey, Boss. Why didn't you tell Viper? He'd want to be here."

"Why do you think? It would destroy him." Boss checked the clip on his semi-automatic. "Doesn't matter. Bain will make it. Move in, clear the buildings."

Boss used hand signals for his men, Rocco, and Viko's crew. They all crept in, weapons drawn, moving into opposite buildings. There was no way they were making a surprise visit in this neck of the woods. As soon as their SUVs pulled up, everyone in these buildings would have noticed.

They had to be on high alert.

Xavier kicked open the wooden door and Killian rushed in, spraying a warning burst against the wall. Boss walked in, slow, steady steps, taking in the surroundings.

His men kept the four men inside covered with firepower. There were a lot of storage boxes haphazardly piled in the corner. He strolled over, lifting the lid of one and peering inside.

"What do we have here?" Boss pulled out a bag of mints. The same style Scarlett had, the ones Bain ate. He threw the bag on the floor in front of the older man, the contents spilling in every direction. "I'm guessing these just arrived from the city. Start talking."

El Diablo brought his gun to the old man's temple. "*Habla, cabrone.*"

"It's not what you think. It wasn't my idea."

Boss paced in front of him, his temper growing. "You created this poison. You know what it does, how it does it, and as far as I'm concerned, all these deaths are on your head."

"If I didn't make more, they'd kill me."

"Who would kill you?" asked Boss. "Names."

He began to shake, piss trickling down his leg. "He'll kill me if I say anything."

Boss nodded to Killian, and a moment later, the old man dropped down to one knee, blood oozing from his pants. He cried out, and the other men cowered back. "Names!"

"Viola. He paid me. It was Viola. He said he was working for Viko and the Circle of Monsters. No one says no to them."

"Where is he now?" asked Boss.

"He left a while ago."

Viko burst in. "The other buildings are full of drugs." Then he saw the scientist on his knee. "You!"

"Viko?"

"You created all this madness?" Viko pulled the old man up by the collar. "I fucked up financing this entire project. Why would you continue it? Why would

Manuel pay you to keep making drugs that kill?"

"He said he was working under your authority."

"He lied."

"I didn't know. I swear I believed you were in charge of this."

The old man was terrified of the Circle of Monsters. Viko obviously had a reputation that preceded him. With that kind of power, there were always opportunists looking to get a slice of the pie. Boss was constantly shutting down anyone stepping out of line on his turf back home.

Viko laughed out loud. "You have no idea what these drugs have cost me, old man."

"Where's the antidote?" asked Boss.

"He wants to make me fall, the little shit." Viko kept ranting, his emotions taking control once again. This time he was sober. "I'll cut off his balls for this."

"Where's the antidote?" Boss repeated, speaking louder this time.

The scientist turned to him. "Gone."

"Gone?"

"He took it for assurance. Even my original notes where I have my formulas."

"Fuck," said Xavier.

"Now what?" asked Killian.

This wasn't good. Manuel knew they were after him and now had what they needed. "Where's Manuel now? How long ago did he leave?"

"An hour or so," said the scientist. "He lives far from here in the city. I swear he gave me no details. I never question him."

Boss ran a hand through his hair as he exhaled his frustration. "Put him in the back of the truck. We're heading to the city. Killian, get Maurice on the fucking phone. I need a location on Viola's cell."

Viko's man had kidnapped the scientist in Colombia, forcing him to make his formula over here where they shipped it out as mints. Without Manuel, without the antidote or formula, Bain's hours were numbered.

****

"*Bastard*," Graciella cursed under her breath for the dozenth time. She was supposed to be tracking the scientist with the "team," not left behind like unwanted trash.

She'd made her way downstairs and found some old wire to use for her handcuffs within minutes. The old warehouse was littered with debris, metal, and old strapping. It had been emptied in a hurry. There were even some valuable tools and machinery that had been left behind in the rush. As she stepped out onto the street, she had no doubt every item of value would be gone by morning.

She wasn't in Kansas anymore.

The neighborhood didn't intimidate her, even if she wasn't dressed for it. She'd grown up in much worse places. Graciella tossed the cuffs and headed down the bustling street. There were people, vendors, and stray dogs everywhere. Familiar smells flooded her senses. Almost immediately, she'd been propositioned and catcalled. And she knew there were men following her. What she needed was a man with a car, preferably one with A/C. Her full leather attire was ill-suited for her current environment and attracting way too much attention.

Graciella unzipped the top of her leather bustier, showing a bit of cleavage. "Can I use your phone?" she asked a guy leaning against a brick wall.

He smiled and passed it to her. Graciella logged into her secure app and checked on the tracker she'd placed on Viko. Widow Maker wasn't a hugger, but it had been the perfect opportunity to tag him. There were audio and GPS she needed to review.

"Sorry, I need to keep this."

She reached into her bra and pulled out her roll of cash, paying him more than the phone was worth. There were so many eyes on her. Flashing money in a place like this wasn't smart for a single woman. But she was too focused on her task to think about it.

All she cared about now was reviewing her app and planning her next move.

Boss drove her crazy. She wanted to kill him and fuck him simultaneously. He'd left her behind, but she'd also double-crossed him by attempting to tag him. Apparently, Viko wasn't as observant in his inebriated state.

She held the phone to her ear as she scanned for a suitable ride.

Manuel Viola? He'd managed to slip away with the antidote. Graciella was in the heart of the city and they were hours away, according to the GPS. She had to act now.

What she needed first was a gun … or preferably gun*s*. Even a knife would do. Thanks to Boss, she had nothing useful on her except the cash she'd kept hidden. She left the main strip and slipped into an alleyway, walking faster. She really needed some shoes without heels.

Her intuition was strong, and she felt their presence before she heard a sound. Graciella bent to adjust her shoe but used the opportunity to size up the three men shadowing her. They were in the alley now, and there was no escape. She didn't even have a purse, so she had no doubt what they wanted from her. Only they weren't going to get it.

There wasn't much alley left, but she stood up and kept walking, scanning the entire area, coming up with her plan.

When she reached the end of the road, she turned and leaned against the brick wall, casually bending one leg up. She didn't utter a word, didn't move, barely breathed.

They smirked, spreading out as they moved in close.

"Hey, baby."

"How about a kiss?" said another.

When they were an arm's length away, she reached out and lightly shoved one in the chest. He laughed out loud at her pitiful attempt to protect herself. What she needed to know was who had the weapons.

"I'll scream," she said.

The guy with the beard chuckled, opening his jacket to reveal a handgun in his waistband. "I'd keep quiet if I were you."

She should try harder when acting, but right now, she couldn't help but smile. Graciella leapt into action, darting forward and snatching the gun before using the heel of her hand against his throat. He staggered back, grasping his neck and wheezing. She shot the first guy in the head and motioned for the third to get to his knees.

"I want every gun, blade, and any ammo you have on the ground," she said. When neither of them made a move to comply, she pistol-whipped the bearded one "Right now!"

Graciella examined her cache of weapons. Now she just needed a ride.

"How far's your car from here?" she asked the man with the facial tattoos.

"Around the block."

"Good. You're my driver now. Get up."

After knocking out the bearded guy, she followed behind her new driver, keeping a gun trained on him. It was a pleasant surprise to find he drove an old El Camino.

They drove to the heart of the city. She did her research on Manuel Viola and continually checked in on Viko with her new cell phone. She was so close to finding the cure and ending this nightmare she could taste it.

"Who runs this town?" she asked.

"I don't know what you're talking about," he said.

"If you want to be a smart ass, I won't think twice about cutting off your dick. I do it all the fucking time. It's kind of my thing."

He believed her. Of course, it wasn't entirely a lie.

"Are you talking about the motorcycle club or the cartel?"

"Cartel."

"Renzo Bianchi controls everything around here from real estate to people. You cross him, you disappear."

"And you work for him?"

"Everyone works for him in one way or another."

She told him the name of the restaurant she wanted, and when he pulled up out front, she stepped out and waved him off. This was Manuel's favorite restaurant, and she knew there was a high likelihood he was inside. She'd seen pics of him online, so now it was time for her to play her role.

Viko and Boss were still a good half-hour away. She couldn't wait. It was time to grasp the opportunity.

Graciella pulled her hair to one side. Normally, when she seduced a man, her makeup was on point and her outfit would make him drool. Today, she'd improvise and use what she had.

Once inside the lavish lobby of the restaurant, she scanned the interior for Manuel. She ignored the hostess, hoping she was right about coming here. When she saw tattoo face and the bearded guy walking up the steps of the restaurant, she cursed under her breath and walked into the heart of the restaurant. The hostess called out to her, but she walked faster, weaving between tables and looking for her mark.

When she caught sight of Manuel, she fought the onslaught of emotions that rushed to the surface from the relief of finding him. This guy had paid the scientist to create more tainted drugs. He had the cure, the only way to end all this death.

He was at a large round table with a bunch of upscale guests. She was only after him, but then she recognized someone else at the table—Renzo Bianchi. Why was Manuel having a meal with the leader of the local cartel if he supposedly wanted to take over? He'd already gone against Viko. Leaders in the underground were never on friendly terms. Trust and comradery weren't the norm, and she doubted it was any different here.

It didn't make sense. Nothing made sense anymore.

Graciella found the ladies' room and freshened up. Her leather outfit was still daring enough to garner attention. If she could avoid those pricks from the alleyway, she may be able to get Manuel alone long enough to find out where he kept the cure. She found a little torture could go a long way in these situations.

She took a deep breath and stepped out of the hallway. Graciella sauntered by the men's table, doing a double-take before leaning over in front of Manuel.

"Manuel, is that you?"

He smiled and the other men at the table approved. "Sorry, I can't recall your name," he said.

Graciella pouted. "That's disappointing. I thought for sure you'd remember me." She ran the tip of her finger along his shoulder.

"Of course," he said. "You should join us."

Everyone began scooting over in an attempt to welcome her to the table, but she whispered in Manuel's ear. "Not here. Just the two of us."

It couldn't have been going better when she noticed the two men from the alley peering in the restaurant, looking for their petty revenge. She was getting over her head, and her nerves were ramping up.

"Tell me when," he said.

"Can I talk to you alone in the hallway for just a minute?" she asked, biting her lower lip for effect. He immediately agreed. She needed to get out of the seating area before she was noticed and her cover blown. Her heart raced.

He followed her back to the hallway near the bathrooms, and just before she turned the corner, she made eye contact with tattoo face. Her entire body tensed. It was only a matter of time now until this all blew up in her face. She had to move fast.

"What was your name again, angel?"

He cupped her face, but she never allowed herself to flinch when on the job. Everything was an act, and she'd perfected the art of tuning out reality to avoid fracturing down the middle.

"Can that be my name?"

"Angel. I like that." He placed a hand on her hip and leaned over to kiss her exposed neck. She closed her eyes, remembering just how much she hated men.

But the kiss never came.

When she blinked open her eyes, there was a knife to his throat. She exhaled the breath she was holding. Then she focused on the large frame behind him. "You'd let another man put his lips on you?"

"You threw me to the wolves."

Boss stared at her, completely tuning out the trembling man under his knife. There was blood all over his hand. When she looked to the right at the other end of the hallway, she saw her two stalkers in a heap against the wall. Sweet relief trickled through her veins. A rush of safety and security she connected with Boss washed over her.

"How'd you find me?"

"There's a tracker on your bra."

She growled. "And here I thought we'd had a moment in your bathroom. I guess I was wrong."

"You weren't wrong."

Graciella narrowed her eyes. "Viko's still twenty minutes out."

"I'm not Viko."

He'd just saved her ass, killing the men after her and rescuing her from this filthy pig. Yes, she could have handled herself as she always had, but it was nice letting it all go. If she ever had a knight in shining armor, it would have been Boss.

"This is Manuel Viola, but I'm sure you already know that," she said.

A bead of blood bubbled up on the man's neck as the blade dug deeper.

"I'm just wondering how far you'd go to get what you want." His tone was thick with jealousy.

She never answered him. Would she have been able to sleep with the enemy? Or would Boss keep creeping into her waking dreams?

Chapter Ten

Manuel Viola was now a dead man and it just so happened, he had the antidote, as hoped. Between Viko and Boss, there was nothing left of the man. She shouldn't have expected anything otherwise. Thankfully, Killian had taken the antidote the moment it had been handed to him and was currently traveling first-class back to Bain. The scientist was also under strict guard and in the process of making a huge batch of the antidote now that he had his notes back. It had been a very productive few days and it wasn't over yet. The drug mints were still making the rounds, and for however long they were killing people, the scientist would need to stay alive. The truth was, right now, she wanted the scientist as dead as Manuel.

She gripped her shoulders, stretching out her neck.

It had been a long few months, a long lifetime.

Graciella closed her eyes, standing perfectly still in her hotel room.

A normal woman would be completely horrified by what she'd just witnessed. Dragging back their one lead to discover all of his secrets. Watching two men, kings in their own right, torture him and make him pay for what he'd done. All of the death was on Manuel's shoulders but the truth was, Graciella was the guilty party. If she hadn't had the stupid idea, so many people would still be alive.

There was no coming away from that.

She released a breath and groaned.

Her body was getting older. So much of her life had been wasted in killing and revenge. It was moments like this she hated herself more than ever.

After all the trouble she'd gone through recently,

she finally had the chance to analyze everything that had happened. It wasn't over, not by a long shot. Manuel hadn't been working alone. The little shit was hot in his pockets of the cartel, which was going to cause a whole load of problems.

"You know it's rude to just sneak into a woman's room," Graciella said. She didn't need to turn around to know Boss was close by.

She'd long given up trying to figure out how he got in. It didn't matter. Even if she locked herself in a tower far away, he'd find her.

"I thought I'd come and see how you were doing."

"Me, I'm fine. Perfectly so. You need to keep an eye on the scientist. He's a slippery little devil."

He chuckled. "Don't worry. I've got additional Killer of Kings watching over him," he said.

He'd gotten closer.

Opening her eyes, she felt him so close to her back. Any other man, she'd have killed him or attacked him, but because it was Boss, he got away with it. He shouldn't be able to get away with anything.

Biting her lip, she didn't move. Didn't lean back.

He was just like other men. There was no way she could allow herself to enjoy him or his company. They were two different people and nothing was going to change that.

"Of course. Daddy says come and your minions come running."

"Now, baby, you're starting to sound a little jealous there."

"Not at all. I'm no minion. I'm a person who can make up my own mind."

Again, his deep rumbling chuckle. Why did he have to sound so good? Why did he even have to feel so good?

"I'm very much aware you've got your own mind, Graciella."

"I'm Graciella now? What happened to Widow Maker? It seems to me, Boss, you pick and choose how and when you want me. It's growing a little tiring." She faked a yawn. "I'm tired now." She covered her mouth and this time, he closed the distance between them so his front touched her back.

Flesh to flesh.

Well, close to flesh. They had their clothes on, but she could still feel his heat.

Why did she have to think of Boss without his clothes on?

His hands went to her arms. She didn't flinch. Didn't pull away.

"You're everything, Graciella. You're the Widow Maker *and* a beautiful woman."

"Don't," she said.

"Why are you so afraid?" he asked.

She turned in his arms and she wished she hadn't. He was so … sexy. It was unfair. Even with his scars, rather than disgusting her, he aroused her.

Emotions she'd long ago promised herself she would never feel came rushing to the surface. Men were monsters. Most men, not all, but still, she'd promised herself she'd never ever feel for anyone. It was safer that way.

Boss wasn't just anyone.

"Why did you have to leave me?" she asked. "I've proven myself time and time again. I don't wear your little groupies' badge but I'm more than capable of handling myself."

"I don't want to talk about this." His hands slid up and down her arms.

"Tough shit. We've all got to do things we don't want to do." This was good. Capturing her anger, feasting on it, meant she wasn't giving in to the need to sink against him. How good would it be to actually let go? To hold on to Boss as if he was some kind of savior? It would be so good.

She wouldn't allow herself to fall. It wouldn't end well.

"You don't trust me, do you? Did you think I was going to run away with the scientist and not let Bain get his precious antidote? You think after all you know about me, I'd do that?" She was under no illusion about her reputation. Ever since this revenge with the drugs had gone horribly wrong, she'd been working her ass off to fix it.

She didn't want more people to die. She'd been working to make sure they were gone from the country. Her biggest mistake was trying to figure it all out herself, she knew that now, more than ever.

From the beginning, she should have gone to Boss. She'd heard about the Killer of Kings years ago, had even watched them and admired their skillset, but she'd never approached, believing she was better off alone.

"It had nothing to do with that." Boss cupped her face. Rather than feel threatened by the touch, she felt comforted, special. She couldn't help but put her hands on his waist, holding him.

Damn it. A simple touch shouldn't feel this good and yet it did.

"Then why? I wanted to help. Can't you see that? Don't you get how important it is for me?" She didn't get the chance to continue as Boss suddenly slammed his lips down on hers.

Kisses meant nothing.

Normally.

There was nothing normal about her and Boss. Far from it. They were fire and ice, and yet together, they smoldered.

Closing her eyes, she moaned as his tongue traced across her bottom lip. After running her hands up his body, she wrapped her arms around his neck and did something she'd never willing done with any other man, she pressed her body against him. She craved his closeness.

One of Boss's hands sank into her hair as the other glided down to grab her ass. The hard ridge of his cock pressed against her, and she whimpered, desperate for more. Heat flooded her pussy. Her mind going from pissed to aroused within a matter of seconds. Only Boss was capable of doing that to her.

As she opened her lips, Boss took the invitation and slid his tongue inside her mouth. She moaned his name, asking for more, wanting more, hungry for it.

He moved them until the wall met her back and she lifted up, wrapping her legs around his waist, riding that wave she was desperate for. Even as she hung off him, Boss propped her up with his body right against the wall.

He broke the kiss. They were both panting. She was as hot for him as he was for her.

Graciella didn't hide her reaction. Didn't care to. Boss was there with her and she was tired of fighting. Tired of constantly trying to be on top, especially when with Boss, she just wanted to be with him, period. There was no need for arguing, no fighting, just complete and utter peace. They could have that. She had no doubt.

"I left you because I didn't want anything to happen to you." He covered her mouth with his hand when she went to argue with him. "You don't think I know how strong, how amazing, how fucking competent you are? I know that. I know you're one hell of a woman, a fantastic assassin, and deep down a very caring and loving woman. You hide it all, and I get it. There is nothing weak about you, Graciella. I'm the weak one."

He removed his hand.

"What? There's nothing weak about you, Boss. You know that. What the hell do you even mean?" She was more than a little confused.

"I should have known you wouldn't understand. When it comes to you, Graciella, you make me weak. I don't think that's necessarily a bad thing." He stroked some of her hair back from her face. "I don't want to be without you, not ever. Yeah, I've thought about killing you when you drive me up the wall, but I wouldn't have it any other way. I want to protect you, always."

Tears filled her eyes as she looked at Boss.

Feelings. For the longest time, she'd hated them. Wanted nothing to do with them. They made her weak. Boss had gotten under her skin and as she kissed him, she knew she couldn't run anymore. Not from him, not from the way he made her feel. She was smitten and there was no turning back.

****

Admitting the truth to Graciella had been easier than Boss expected.

He wasn't lying to her. He didn't want her to ever get hurt. Her past still clung to her like a second skin and all he wanted to do was to tear down the past, to show her a life with him wouldn't cause her any more pain.

"Graciella?" he asked.

"Tonight," she said, pulling away.

Her lips were swollen.

"Tonight?"

"Yes, you and me. Nothing else. Please. You're

not the king and I'm not the competition. We're just Graciella and Boss. Two people who met. No promises. Can we do that?"

He wasn't looking for a one-night stand, far from it, but with Graciella, he was more than willing to give her what she wanted.

Running his hand down her back, going to her ass again, he stepped back.

"Boss?"

He pulled his shirt over his head, throwing it to one side. He had two guns tucked into his jeans, and he put them on the chest of drawers beside the wall. Next, he rid himself of his pants and looked at her, standing in just his black boxer briefs.

"You approve?"

She licked her lips. "You're a beast."

Her fingers teased the edge of her shirt. He could have taken off her clothes, but this was for her. If she wanted to stop, they'd stop. He'd never force her, not once.

Boss waited with bated breath as she waited.

This was a tease.

She lifted her shirt over her head, showing her padded bra, but also that she carried just as many weapons as he did. She placed hers beside his and next worked on her jeans. Wriggling out of them, she stood in her underwear.

They were both without weapons.

Vulnerable.

Both at each other's mercy.

Rather than wait for Graciella to take the next step because she'd already gone out of her comfort zone, he put a hand at her waist and pulled her close. "Tell me to stop."

"No."

"Damn it, Graciella."

"I want this, Boss." She put her hand to his chest and slowly slid it down until she covered his boxer briefs. "I love the fact you wear black." She squeezed him. "If you don't want to, back away."

In answer, he took possession of her mouth. There was no way he didn't want to. He moved them away from the wall and took her to the bed. Slowly, he lowered her onto the top, still kissing her.

Stroking down her body, he went to her knees, holding them open.

"Don't worry. I know it's you. I won't panic," she said. "Please, Boss."

He knew her history like no one else. She was safe with him. "I haven't even gotten started." He kissed her neck, flicking his tongue across her pulse. She let out a gasp and now he used his teeth to create the perfect level of pain and then soothe it out with light flicks.

Down he went, going to the tops of her breasts. He kissed each mound before reaching behind her to flick the catch of her bra open. Sliding the straps down her arms, he removed it from her body to stare at her.

"Do you even realize how fucking beautiful you are?" he asked. He saw the blush in her cheeks and couldn't help but smile. "I take it from that look you don't have a clue."

"Why don't you show me?"

"Gladly."

His tongue flicked over one beaded nipple before taking the second one into his mouth. She arched up, moaning his name. The sound filled the room, echoing off the walls.

He cupped both tits and teased each bud before biting down then sucking them into his mouth. They were more than a generous mouthful. He wanted them swaying in front of him as he fucked her. Damn it, he just wanted Graciella forever.

Slowly, he trailed his lips down her body, going to her stomach, then lower. The panties still covered her pussy and that was where he wanted to be.

Pressing his face against the fabric covering her cunt, he breathed her in. She released a little cry. The sound so sweet yet shocking. He couldn't get enough of her, didn't want to.

The panties were now an obstruction. Gripping the crotch, he pulled. The seams were no match for his strength. They came apart with ease. He threw the offending item away. Now he got to see her pretty pussy.

She was already wet but he intended to make her even more so.

Sliding the lips of her pussy open, he looked at her sweet, swollen clit. He wanted his dick inside her, to taste her, to drown in this woman. Putting the flat of his tongue to her clit, he stroked back and forth.

"Oh my fucking God!" Graciella's pleasured moans filled the air. He stopped long enough to look at her, and fuck, if she wasn't a sight to behold. So beautiful. So sexy. So amazing.

Licking her clit, he tugged it into his mouth with a groan. He bit down, making her writhe beneath him, just so perfect and open. Her desperate mewling made his cock rock-hard. He teased back and forth with his tongue then moved down to stroke along her slit.

"You're killing me," she cried.

He pressed his hands to her inner thighs, keeping her open as he started to thrust inside her, plunging in deep with his tongue. Then he returned to her clit, determined to devote plenty of attention to that sweet little bud. He could stay between her legs half the night.

She wriggled beneath him and he rubbed his face

against her, not wanting to let go. He wanted her to know real pleasure, from a man who demanded nothing in return. Her cream coated his face and he lapped it up. She was about to peak, thrusting her pussy against his face, gasping and tensing. He cupped her ass cheeks, holding her close as he nibbled mercilessly on her pussy.

"Yes, please, yes," she said. "I'm close, Boss. So close."

"Come for me, princess."

She did.

He swallowed down her cum as she let go and it was so fucking beautiful. Boss didn't stop there, letting her ride her wave of pleasure, more than happy to be the one to give her an orgasm. Only when she settled down from her peak did he slow down, giving her time to enjoy the bliss.

He reached into his night table, retrieving a condom. From the tip down, he worked on the latex, the head of his cock already leaking pre-cum as he wanted inside her.

"Tell me to stop, Graciella. Tell me you don't want me."

She wrapped her arms around his neck and smiled up at him. "Boss, fuck me. Fuck me like you mean it."

He growled and slammed his lips down on hers. She was pure sin and he couldn't deny her anything. Didn't want to. Holding her legs open with his hips, he rested the tip of his cock at her opening, staring into her eyes, waiting.

"You've got to put me inside you," he said.

Every single step was going to be her accepting him, giving it to him. He'd never force her. If she wanted him, she was going to show him just how much.

With his cock at her entrance, he watched,

entranced as she reached down between them. She took his cock in her hand. Thick and swollen, he wanted to get rid of the condom, to feel her skin to skin, but there would be time for that.

She eased the mushroom head against her clit, bumping it, and he groaned as she arched up, moaning as she did. So pretty. So perfect. Everything he ever wanted.

"That's right, princess. Use me. Take what you want and fucking love it."

She moved his cock down to her opening and with her gaze on him, she slowly pulled him inside.

Graciella was hot, tight, and it took every ounce of control for him to not push her hands out of the way and fuck her hard and fast. He wanted to pat himself on the back for not fucking her harder than ever before. This night was something new for both of them. It meant more than cheap thrills or a contract fulfilled. It was real. Lasting.

When his pelvis hit her hand, she let go. Her hands went to his ass and pulled him in those last few inches.

"God, you're big, Boss. I knew you'd be good, but not this good."

"I'm all yours now."

To help her, he thrust, securing himself deep within her.

She gasped and he kissed her, swallowing down any more moans. He held perfectly still within her. Not just to let her get accustomed to his dick, but also for him to gain control. The last thing he wanted to do was let go like some teenage boy.

He was so close.

Graciella was everything. He'd known the moment he met her she would be his. He just didn't realize how much she'd fuck with his head. There was no way he'd never be able to let her go.

As he stared down at her, she licked her lips and offered him the sweetest smile.

"I'm not … there's no game here, Boss. It's just me," she said. "I promise. I swear it."

"You've got all of me as well, baby. I'm not playing a game. I'm just me." He started to pull out of her until only the tip of him remained. He watched her, waiting for any sign that this was too much for her. She'd been through things no woman should ever be subjected to.

She gave no sign she wanted this to stop, so he thrust within her tight heat, loving her moans. He would only ever give her pleasure. All he wanted was for her to let go with him—no act, no worries.

He could give her a damn good life that she'd only ever dreamed of. He'd give her the world if she let him.

Thrusting inside her, he started off slow, not wanting to rush this. He glanced down and watched his cock. The condom an annoyance but necessary.

Groaning, he couldn't resist teasing her clit, bringing her to a second orgasm as he drove inside her, feeling her spasm around him.

He was nearly there. There was no holding back.

Taking her hands, he pressed them down at either side of her head, kissing her lips as he rode her pussy, feeling the first stirrings of his orgasm as he filled her, flooding the condom with his release. The pleasure didn't end there. It slowly ebbed away and Boss knew he was never going to be the same again. Whatever happened, he couldn't let Graciella go. No more running away. She was part of him, and because of that, her problems were now his. He'd protect her, die for her. All that remained now was to marry her.

Chapter Eleven

One week later

It felt good to be back in the city. *Her city.* For the first time in forever, she had no desire to run. A huge weight had been lifted off her shoulders now that an antidote for the drugs had been found. Manuel Viola was dead. The scientist was under lock and key until Boss decided otherwise. Bain had recovered. Her nightmare was finally over.

It felt odd not having that guilt clinging to her like a shadow. It had crept up on her each morning and didn't let her sleep at night. She was free from the burden of her mistake all those years ago. The only thing left on her mind was the debt to Viko. That would never be repaid. It would never allow her to have a fresh start. How could she even contemplate a relationship with Boss when she had a debt with his enemy?

She'd been avoiding Boss the past week.

Once they were home, she second-guessed the night they shared together. Many people indulged when on vacation and lived to regret it. Although they hadn't been in the Dominican for rest and relaxation, it was a different place, a unique reality.

Boss could have any woman he wanted—young women, virgins, women with no scars and baggage. He was a man of power and wealth.

She couldn't give him heirs. Her body was broken. It would almost be cruel to subject him to a life with her when he could have so much more.

It had been a nice fantasy while it lasted.

Then why couldn't she stop thinking about him?

Graciella rolled over in her bed, grabbing her cell phone from the nightside table. She exhaled her disappointment.

"What do you want, Viko?"

"You were much more respectful when you needed my money and support. You have a short memory."

"Well, I doubt you're calling to chitchat."

"You're right. And you're going to help me."

"Do you expect me to be your errand girl for the rest of my life?"

He laughed. "The burden of being in debt. I don't recommend it."

"Yeah, thanks."

She dropped back on her bed, draping an arm over her eyes. This would be a nightmare that never ended.

"Manuel screwed me over. He wanted my place in the Circle. He's dead, but I know he wasn't working alone. There was no way he could fund the manufacturing and exporting of those drugs on his own."

"What do you expect me to do?" she asked.

"You're one of the best. You speak the language. And, as I've mentioned, you owe this to me. Go back to the Dominican. Fuck whoever you need to fuck. I need to know who's out to get me."

She felt sick to her stomach thinking about Viko meddling in her life forever, not allowing her to move on and put the past behind her. She liked working solo, having no one to answer to but herself.

Graciella had to start her day. After a quick shower, she headed out of her condo. There was a black SUV with heavily tinted windows parked outside on the street. The glass began to lower. "Get in."

She barely recognized this guy. "Who's asking?"

"You have a date with Boss in fifteen minutes. He doesn't like to be kept waiting."

Graciella wanted to tell the driver to fuck off, but

instead, she got into the vehicle. She was curious about what he wanted from her. And she had nothing better to do than head to the coffee shop for a latte.

"I thought Killian was his driver."

"I'm Chains, if you don't remember me. I've been driving Boss around a lot longer than Killian."

She remembered Xavier talking about his good friend Chains. Her nerves settled.

"And where is this date?"

"Breakfast on the water. Five-star patio. Their croissants were featured in *Food Addiction* magazine last month."

"Wow, that's a lot more detail than I was expecting." She leaned back and watched the city flash by. The Killer of Kings men were unlike any other hitmen she'd worked with in the past.

They pulled up to the restaurant and she stepped out. Boss was already seated, and he waved her over. She couldn't help but smile. He looked so pleased with himself.

"Kidnapping me won't get you any points."

"You haven't answered my calls," he said.

"I've been busy."

He used a hand to motion her to sit. It was a two-person table overlooking the water. There were three fresh roses in the vase—red, yellow, and white. She had to admit she was impressed. Her breakfasts weren't nearly as extravagant or involved.

"You've been avoiding me, Graciella. Why?"

She took a breath, not willing to play games at this point. She was tired, soul deep. "I don't want to be the flavor of the week. I know how this ends," she said. "I was hoping you'd have a new conquest by now."

He narrowed his eyes, taking a sip of his coffee, nodding her to drink her own.

"Your brother still won't drink coffee, did you know that? Old wounds never heal for some. Then there are others, like you, who seem unfazed."

She tasted her coffee. "What you see isn't always what you get. My brother has his wounds, I have mine. We deal with things in our own way."

"And you like to run. To put up walls so high that nobody can get in."

She shrugged, taking another sip. "If it works…"

Boss leaned back in his seat, staring at her. Seagulls cawed over the water. A boat horn bellowed in the distance. This place reminded her of her own little hideaway by the ocean. It relaxed her.

"You're not the flavor of the week, Graciella. I'm done with other women. There's only one I'm interested in."

"When you say that, I feel threatened."

"I know. You need to learn to trust me. I won't hurt you," he said. "No one knows your story like I do. I'm still here, baby. And I'm not running."

God, she wanted Boss. He looked so damn edible. He was a tattooed, muscular beast sitting on an overpriced restaurant patio and no one dared tell him he didn't belong. He was the kind of man who demanded respect and got what he wanted.

He reached into his jacket and pulled out an elaborate ring box. He placed it on the table then pushed it toward her. She stared, not knowing what to think. He hadn't said a word.

Graciella decided to put it all on the line since he'd convinced himself he wanted her.

"Have you forgotten my debt to Viko? I imagine a man like you would bristle knowing their woman owed a lifetime debt to the Circle of Monsters."

He tapped his fingers on the table, not speaking,

his eyes intense.

"Exactly. A deal breaker," she said.

"Open the damn box, Graciella."

She took a breath and reached for the box. He placed his hand briefly over hers, startling her, then he sat back and waited.

Was she holding her breath? It felt like the entire world had slowed down just for this moment. She opened the box. Inside was the largest, most perfect diamond engagement ring she'd ever seen. And she'd seen a lot in her line of work. This was something else entirely.

"I commissioned it just for you," he said.

She swallowed hard. "What does this mean?"

Boss leaned over the table, holding her forearm in place as she held the box with the other. "Marry me, Graciella. We have one life to live. We've both suffered enough. Why can't we be happy? Together."

"Marriage? The killer of kings is asking me to marry him?"

She was dumbfounded and all her thoughts and higher reasoning went out the window, leaving her helpless and unsure of what to say next.

"Why not?"

"I can write a list a mile long why it wouldn't work," she said, staring at the ring.

"But it'll work in spite of it all. Because I love you."

This time, she looked him in the eyes, completely taken aback. She'd always felt so unlovable that it felt foreign to hear it—and believe it.

"Boss…"

"Marry me, Graciella Moreno. I swear to God, I'll be true to you for the rest of my days."

Her first instinct was to run, to refuse all the beautiful words. But he was right. Enough was enough.

She didn't think she was capable of it after everything she'd been through, but she loved him too. He drove her crazy and she loved him anyway.

She thought about him all the time.

Even now, she couldn't help but remember their first time a week ago. Despite all the bullshit she'd endured in her life, he made her feel feminine, desirable, like she'd never known a man before him.

How could she walk away from that?

"Can we be alone?"

He rose an eyebrow. "When? Now?"

"Now."

Boss raised one arm to request the bill.

They walked toward the cars in the lot. "Did you drive here yourself?" she asked. "Or did Chains drop you off?"

"He's a good man. I wouldn't have sent him to pick you up if I didn't trust him." Boss pushed his key fob and a navy-blue BMW chirped a few feet away. "And I do drive myself at times."

"You're full of surprises today," she said, stepping into the passenger seat of his car.

****

She hadn't said *yes*. Boss felt like a schoolboy vying for a girl's attention. He wouldn't go to sleep tonight until he had his answer.

He drove them to one of his many properties. The penthouse suite of this hotel was where he did a lot of business. It also had the best view of the city.

"Where are we?" she asked, entering the luxury condo.

"One of my offices. You like it?"

He watched Graciella as she made her way to the floor-to-ceiling windows. The woman knew how to move, how to use her body to drive men crazy. He wasn't immune.

"I thought my condo had a good view, but this … this is unbelievable." She pressed a hand to the glass, taking in the views.

He came up behind her and wrapped his arms around her waist. "I have a lot of things. More money than I can ever spend. Every toy and gadget a man could want. There's one thing I've learned during all these years."

She turned to face him, wrapping her arms around his neck. "What's that, Boss?"

"Money can't buy happiness."

Graciella narrowed her eyes. "So they say. That's a common expression."

"No, it's true. *Things* can't stave off loneliness."

"How can the great Boss ever be lonely? You could be surrounded by new people day and night and they'd beg for your company."

"Then they go home. I need more, Graciella. Life is empty without love. After watching so many of my men get married, I always wondered what the fascination was—until you came along."

"I'm nothing special," she said.

"You're everything to me," he said. He kissed her forehead. "You never answered my question."

She shook her head. "My debt, Boss. It won't go away."

"I know you talked to Viko this morning."

"Of course, you do."

"He's paranoid. Everything's falling down around him."

Ever since finding out his man Manuel had double-crossed him, he'd been on a killing spree. The devil in him had been released and couldn't be contained.

"Since he thinks of me as his personal slave, I

guess I'll be going down with him."

"I'll never let that happen," he said. "You know who Manuel was working with in the cartel?"

She nodded.

"Don't tell Viko. I'm going to make him a deal he can't refuse."

Graciella cocked her head. "What are you up to, Boss?" She ran her fingers through his hair.

"I want you to be mine, only mine," he said.

"You want to own me."

He growled. "Call it what you will. It works both ways."

"Are you telling me you'll never crave your weekly specials?"

Graciella was jealous to a fault. She believed she had reason, but Boss had never been more sincere. Just thinking about all those nameless whores made his stomach churn.

"That's exactly what I'm telling you. A king is nothing without his queen."

She smiled at that.

"You're the best at everything, or so they say. Prove it to me."

"Last week wasn't enough?"

"This time I'll keep score."

This woman drove him wild. She wasn't afraid of him and didn't hold back her thoughts. It fucking turned him on to have a strong woman put him in his place. Of course, he let Graciella get away with murder. No other person pushed his buttons and lived to tell about it.

He leaned in and kissed her. The room was soundproofed, leaving only the sounds of their breathing. She began stripping herself, not breaking the kiss. When she pulled back, she was only in her bra and panties.

"Take your shirt off," she said. "I want to touch

you."

Boss tugged his shirt off and slipped out of his shoulder harness, placing them on his desk.

"Let's play a game," she said.

"Okay."

She ran her fingers down his chest and along his six-pack. "Where'd you get this scar?"

He looked down at one of the gashes on his stomach. It took him a minute to even remember there were so many damn scars. "Shrapnel wound. I had to cut it out myself. Is it my turn?"

She nodded.

He kissed his way down her body until he was on one knee. Boss rubbed his face against her panties, making her jolt. Then he touched a deep scar on her lower stomach. "Where's this from?"

Her body tensed.

"They wanted to be sure I'd never get pregnant. Pregnant girls were a liability."

"Fuck this game," he said, scooping her up into his arms. "No one will hurt you again."

He'd had enough of the sadness, the guilt, the shame. Nothing from her past could surprise him or make his feelings change. All he wanted to do was make his woman happy.

He settled her down on his grand oak desk overlooking the skyline. "That doesn't bother you? Never having an heir?"

"Baby, if I wanted kids, I'd have kids. Killer of Kings is my legacy. All I want is the gorgeous woman in front of me. You're all I need and want."

He spread her legs and leaned over her body, kissing her neck, rimming the shell of her ear. He undid her bra and slid off her panties. Having Widow Maker sprawled naked over his desk was a beautiful sight. He'd never get tired of fucking her.

"Let me see you," she said.

He stepped out of his pants and boxers. Boss had nothing to hide. He stroked his erection a couple of times while she watched. His cock was thick and long and he had the stamina to go all night. "You want this inside you?"

She looked spellbound, her eyes already glazed over with lust. "Fuck me, Boss. I want to feel it tomorrow."

He groaned. Forget sugar and spice. His Latina queen was filthy as fuck. He bent down and feasted on her clit, occasionally licking up her folds. She writhed on his desk, his paperwork and ornaments falling to the ground.

"Scream all you want, baby. Nobody can hear you." He tugged her hips to the edge of the desk, then wasted no time sinking deep in her hot cunt. "Fuck, you feel perfect around my cock."

She mewled and wiggled, hungry for him to work her body.

"Such a naughty girl." He fucked her at a slow rhythm, watching himself fill her over and over again. "You need to be taught some fucking manners."

"Yes, I've been bad," she said. "Punish me."

He picked up the tempo, fucking her deep and hard, the desk scraping along the tiles. With Graciella, it was a challenge to hold back and not spill inside her. She was so damn sexy.

Boss flipped her over, impaling her with his cock right away. She cried out, her hands clutching the edges of the desk. "More!"

He grabbed a handful of her long black hair, his other hand securing her hip. He gave her a few firm slaps to spur her on. Boss rammed into her body, her ass jiggling, her breasts pressed against his desk. She cried out, the erotic sound music to his ears.

"Take my ass." She was insatiable. Unlike any woman he'd ever taken before. "I want you everywhere. Only you."

He wasn't prepared for any of this. The last thing he wanted to do was hurt her, but she was insistent. He used the cream from her pussy and dragged it to her asshole, coating the cute little rosette in moisture.

Pre-cum leaked at the end of his cock. He'd never been so fucking horny in his life. He pressed the head of his erection at that forbidden hole, pushing in slow and steady. She growled, pushing back against him, filling herself with dick.

"You're absolutely perfect." He looked down between them, his cock deep in her ass. He ran both palms from her shoulders all the way down her body until he reached her hips. Boss began to piston in and out of her ass. He used one hand around her body to tease her clit, rubbing her in quick circles. The dual stimulation made her moans deepen, the sounds making it near impossible to hold off much longer.

"Come for me, baby. Be a good girl and milk my cock."

She let out a series of mini gasps before finally letting go, crying out with pleasure. Boss held on tight and filled her ass with his cum. Once their breathing settled, he hoisted her dead weight into his arms. She wouldn't even open her eyes.

He set her down on his bathroom counter and used a damp facecloth to clean them both up. As he was finishing up, she watched him. A calm, natural beauty on her face. No guises.

Boss stood in front of her and cupped her face, kissing her lips once, twice.

"You're worried about me, but should I be worried? You're the Widow Maker, known for being a man bait. Maybe I'm the one being used."

"Don't worry about me, Boss." Her smile was sad. "Everything here, between you and me, it's the first time I've been real in as long as I can remember. I feel safe with you." Her eyes filled with moisture. When she blinked, a few tears traced down her cheeks.

"That's how it should be." He kissed her tears then brought his forehead to hers. "I'll never let anyone hurt you."

"You didn't use a condom."

"No."

They stayed like that, connected on a deeper level. Comfortable in each other's presence. Real, naked, vulnerable, and experiencing love for the first time.

"Boss?"

"Yeah, baby."

"Do you think this can work?" she whispered.

"It will work. Before you came along, I couldn't understand the fascination with settling down with one woman. I berated my men about it. Even Xavier. Now all I can think about is making you happy."

"Can I see that ring again?"

He pulled on some boxers and got the ring from his jacket pocket. He sat on the leather sofa and patted his lap. Graciella hadn't put on any clothes and he couldn't complain. She sat on his lap and opened the box.

Boss took the ring out. It had cost him a small fortune. He took her left hand and slipped it onto her ring finger. It fit perfectly, made just for her.

"Wow." She held her hand up to the light, tilting in this way and that to see the sparkle.

"Did I pass the test?" he asked.

Graciella smirked then cupped his face with one hand, giving him a kiss. It was soft, sweet, and full of promises. "Yes, and I'll marry you, Boss."

Chapter Twelve

No woman had ever gotten under his skin before. Rather than see it as a weakness and curse, Boss saw it as a strength and prospect for the future. He wouldn't let another moment slip through his fingers.

It was why he was here, sitting in an unfamiliar chair smoking one of Viko's cigars again. He hated the taste of them. The home itself was in a secure location on a private island just off the coast. Viko apparently liked the best of everything. And his privacy.

Ever since Viko had given Graciella the mission of obtaining the man responsible for funding the distribution of the drugs, he'd gone into some kind of hiding. Either that, or he really intended to stay out of the way.

Boss made it his mission to find out how people lived, certainly when it came to his competition or enemies. The Circle of Monsters was nothing more than a bunch of highly paid thugs. He didn't like them, didn't respect them. They weren't the kind of people he'd hire for delicate missions. If he wanted to make a scene to get the job done, sure. Viko could certainly rally up his men and create a shitstorm.

Personally, Boss liked to play the game. He was a man of many faces.

When he started Killer of Kings, he'd done so with the intent of being the best, of hiring the best. The only way he knew how to survive was to be the best. To fight harder, to be stronger, and to be more patient than everyone

Where he believed revenge was a dish best served cold, Viko was fire and reaction. It was why the Circle of Monsters would never best Killer of Kings, and possibly why in the scheme of things, they were, for all intents and purposes, evenly matched. Still, Boss wouldn't be on friendly terms any time soon. Not with Viko, not with the men he associated with.

"I'm starting to think you're after my ass, Boss," Viko said. "Multiple secret meetings all in one month. I feel special."

"You shouldn't."

"Have you come to finally even the score? Want to try and kill me?"

"I don't have any desire to kill you, Viko. Don't give a fuck about hurting you at all." He blew a ring of smoke up into the air. He'd only taken a couple of puffs of the thing but he was done. He crushed it down on Viko's desk. "Do you run away all the time?"

Viko threw his head back and laughed. "You think this is running?"

"You didn't get what you wanted and rather than stay and fight for it like a real man, you're here doing whatever it is you have to do. So yeah, I think you're running. Do I scare you?" Boss asked.

"Why don't you worry more about getting your woman down the aisle than what I'm doing with my time?"

Boss smiled.

"Do you think you're the only person in this world who can gather information about your opponent?"

"Not really. It's no secret I intend to marry the Widow Maker."

"Let's hope her namesake doesn't follow you into the bedroom, Boss. You might not be able to come out alive."

"It's sweet that you care," said Boss. "I'm not here for any reason other than to deal with this debt you've got going on with my woman."

"What Graciella owes me is between the two of

us." Viko folded his arms across his chest.

To any casual observer, they were merely two men, no weapons, but Boss knew Viko just as Viko knew him. They had weapons on them, but kept them hidden in the most convenient of places.

"Graciella is mine. She belongs to me and will eventually become part of the Killer of Kings."

Viko's insane laughter echoed around the room. "Okay, now I know you're crazy. Do you really think that woman has what it takes to run an empire as stoic as Killer of Kings? Damn, you're going to be down when it comes to business. Graciella will run you guys into the ground. First, she doesn't take orders from anyone."

"What do you call what she does for you then?"

"Oh, I give her orders but she doesn't follow them. You're alive, aren't you?"

Boss folded his arms. As with all meetings with Viko, he was starting to grow bored. This was getting them nowhere. "I've long ago accepted that I won't kill you, Viko. We're too evenly matched and regardless of what I think of your little organization, you actually do the right thing. The good thing."

"Aw, are you getting all sentimental in your old age, Boss?"

"I'll give you Renzo Bianchi. He's the man you want. In return, you grant me Graciella's freedom." He took a step from behind the desk. He was done playing nice. "You will never call on her. Never ask her for help. You will leave her alone. Free and clear. As far as you're concerned, Graciella, Widow Maker, or whatever it is you fucking call her doesn't exist. She is free to be with me." He wasn't smiling anymore. Too much was at stake.

He didn't come here to banter with Viko.

This bastard had already spent too much time

sharing the same air as him.

Viko chuckled. "You really expect me to believe that? You're going to give me a cartel in exchange for a piece of pussy you've already fucked?"

"Be careful," he said. "My offer ends in a matter of minutes and I want you to think carefully before you give me an answer. It's a limited offer, but if you decide to make this difficult for Graciella or me, then I will personally see to it that Renzo has the best life money can buy. He'll never suffer a day in his life. Other than funding the drugs and running a cartel, he's kind of like a stand-up guy. Everyone who died from taking those drugs, they're collateral damage."

He stared at Viko, waiting, then he continued, "If that's not enough to persuade you, we're evenly matched, but your boys aren't. Where they go, I'll be there. I'll become your biggest fucking nightmare. Business will be affected. I guarantee it. In fact, I even look forward to the prospect of ruining you and running Circle of Monsters into the ground. All you've got to do is grant Graciella her freedom, and I will personally hand you Renzo. You'll have your peace." It didn't matter to him what happened to the bastard. Bain had nearly died because of the drugs.

He would see it through if Viko made the wrong choice.

Silence stretched out.

To anyone else, this would make for an uncomfortable debate, for Boss, this was where he was most comfortable. No one could best him. Not even Viko.

"What if I need the Widow Maker's expertise?" Viko asked, surprising him. "She's rare, Boss. Take away her owing me, she's still damn good at what she does."

"Simple, you come to me. You need her for an assassin, I'll be the one you call. Under no circumstances will she be selling herself. Her body is mine. Every part of her belongs to me."

"Damn, brought down by a woman."

Boss chuckled without humor. "Not at all. I can still walk away from you and take my little peace offering with me. I'm not weak, Viko. I'm right where I'm supposed to be. You want to see weak, look in the mirror. You've allowed your emotions to cloud your judgment one too many times. You could have taken Renzo, but your thirst for revenge kept it from you." He shrugged. "What's it going to be? Island life is starting to irritate me."

Viko looked at him, his features set. Boss knew damn well he'd hit his hot buttons.

"You knew I'd take the deal. I don't even know what you're still doing here. Until Renzo is in my hands, I can still call for Graciella."

Boss approached him and slammed the key against his chest. "He's tied to your bed, waiting for whatever you want to give him."

Viko caught the key as Boss moved away, heading for the door.

"You knew I'd take the deal?" Viko asked.

Boss glanced back. "The drugs killed your kid. I didn't doubt for a second that you wouldn't take the deal. I've never known that kind of pain. I can only begin to imagine how this case has been for you."

"I hope for your sake you never feel it," Viko said.

"Well, I hope for you, when you've done with Renzo, you'll find some kind of peace, any peace." Boss turned and left. He didn't look back. There was no need to. Bain was still waiting for him in the boat. The big fucker had lost a little too much weight during his illness and from what his informants said, he kept hitting the gym and eating like there was no tomorrow.

"Did you get what you needed to?" Bain asked.

"Yes, let's head home." Renzo was going to die. By his hand or Viko's, it didn't really matter. He found an opportunity to save his woman and he took it. When it came to Graciella, he would do everything for her. She owned his heart, and he intended to show her a world full of love, and a whole lot of killing.

****

One month later

It had been a long time since Graciella had worn white. She stared at her reflection and her nerves were completely shot. This wasn't supposed to be her life, but here she was, living the dream.

Her wedding day.

How had it arrived so fast? There was no time to escape. No way for her to leave, not that she wanted to either. No, in the past month, Boss had shown her a place in his world, and it worked. She wanted to be with him every day. Killer of Kings was an empire with so many intricate details and went so deep into all parts of the world. She had underestimated the sheer size of it.

No wonder Boss controlled it with an iron fist. She never thought she'd be part of something so amazing, so powerful. It felt good to belong. They were all just cogs in a much bigger network, but without it, she hated to even think of what the world could be like.

There was a knock at the door and she called for them to come in. The other Killer of Kings women were so nice but Graciella didn't exactly know her place with them. They were good girls and they had little in common. It was still a sore subject for her and a constant struggle to find her place among them. Time would help.

One day, she'd become accustomed to not being alone in the world.

Twirling, she spun out the skirt.

"You look beautiful," Xavier said, catching her off guard.

She'd been successfully avoiding her brother for a long time. Until now. She turned toward him. "You think so?"

"You do and you know it."

"I don't know. I'm not used to being the star of the show. I've been to many weddings. Some of them have ended in blood baths. That's the way the world goes. Hopefully Boss and I will get to say the *I do* before then." She rambled. Why was she so nervous? She pushed some of her hair out of her face.

"I know we're never going to be where we were as kids. Too much shit has happened. We both have different lives now." He stopped. "I'll always be the brother who didn't protect you and that will stay—"

"Right, stop." She held up her hand. "I didn't want to do this but I don't blame you, Xavier. I really don't. You're my brother, sure, and the whole brothers protect their sisters, I get it. We were both kids. Both of us, not just me. You were a kid as well, and I will not allow you to carry this guilt. It's not yours to carry. You didn't sell me or hurt me. Our lives took unexpected turns and I dealt with it."

She took a deep breath. "Just stop feeling guilty about what happened and move on. It's all we can really do. I don't want you to be here because you feel like you have some kind of debt to me. I'm in love with Boss and that's scary enough. He's a crazy guy and amazing, and I can't believe how lucky I am that despite everything we've gone through, he's going to marry me today. I'm happy, Xavier. Against all odds, I'm happy. I know you're happy too. I'm going to be an aunt. You'll be a daddy, a damn good one. What's more, every time you see me, I don't want you to be thinking about what you couldn't do as kids. I don't want to keep being reminded of what was taken from us, Xavier. Our childhoods were stolen from us. Stop trying to steal the chance that we have now as adults."

Xavier nodded. "I can do that."

"Good, because I didn't ask you this as I knew you'd cry on me. Will you walk me down the aisle to your boss?" she asked, smiling. He was the only family she had, so it was only fitting.

"Of course, I'll walk my sister down the aisle. It'll be an honor. And he's more than just my boss. He's also a friend." He held out his arm. "By the way, I don't cry."

"I can see a tear. It's right there. You just got to blink and it will slip right down your cheek."

"You know what your couple's nickname will be?"

"Nickname?" she asked.

"Yeah, like Brangelina. Graciella and Boss, so it'll be Gross. I totally agree. The thought of you two together makes me nauseous."

"Xavier, act your age." She shook her head.

He chuckled. "I really hope Boss can handle you."

"He'll never be able to handle me, but it's going to be fun to see him try."

Graciella didn't want to get married in a church or at the city hall. Instead, she'd asked if they could rent a villa near the ocean so they could have their wedding on the beach. She didn't expect Boss to own an island or for a priest to be one of the Killer of Kings. That was his name, Priest. He didn't go by any other name, and she'd yet to hear him speak. Half his face had tattoos, and there was nothing holy about the man.

Boss had his secrets but she knew he was all hers. She had fought him for so long but there was no one else she wanted more. Men had torn her life to shreds, but Boss was determined to put her back together piece by piece. He was her knight in shining armor.

The music started. A small band on the edge of their group sounded like an orchestra. It was incredible. Other Killer of Kings men and their wives were present. Their intimate group of people. This was where she belonged. She didn't have to run anymore.

Everyone else faded away. All her focus was on the beast of a man in front of her. The man who'd been able to shatter her cold heart and make her hope for a better life, to make her feel true love.

Xavier placed her hand within Boss's and as he moved to stand beside her, Priest started to talk. His gruff voice garnered everyone's attention.

She didn't move. She only had eyes for Boss.

Ever since she was taken, she'd stopped believing in fairy tales. They were just stories kids told themselves. There was never a handsome prince to save you. For the longest time, she had only been able to rely on herself.

Boss was her prince. She saw it now.

With him, she knew deep down she could experience life how it should be.

"Graciella, I will make sure you never regret a moment of being with me. I intend to love, cherish, and help guide you into being the perfect wife for me." She chuckled as he winked at her. "Meeting you, finding you, it made me realize there's no one in this world I want more. You blew my entire world apart and I craved it, wanted it, was desperate for a piece of you, any part of you I could take. I'll love you more than anything else in this world."

Tears filled her eyes but she didn't let them spill. He slid the ring onto her finger and she reached for his ring.

"Boss, I never thought I'd be able to believe in love, let alone experience it. When I'm with you, I realize I've only been existing. You give me a reason, a purpose to live. I can't guarantee you our life will be perfect, but it will be pretty damn close." She laughed. "I'm really not good with speeches."

Their small crowd laughed. Boss ran his thumb across her knuckles. Priest continued and when he got to the part of kissing her, she was more than happy.

Boss cupped her cheek, brought her close, and his lips covered hers. At that moment, she knew she had made the right choice. There was no one else in this world who had ever come close to making her feel like this. He was everything she could ever want and more.

Their friends cheered for them. Boss wasn't finished. Both of his hands were on her face, and she wrapped her arms around him, forgetting about their small crowd, getting as close as she could to him.

"I love you, Graciella."

"And I love you, Boss. You're never getting rid of me. I hope you can handle that."

His hands moved down her back, going toward her ass as he pulled her in tight. Their bodies completely flush together, she felt the hardness of his cock. "I can handle everything you dish out."

"Good, because I don't feel like dancing, eating, or mingling. Can we go back to our villa? Because I want to make use of every room in it. Let's make our wedding night the start of our whole new life together."

Without thanking any of them, Boss scooped her up into his arms and laughed as he carried her across the sand just like the fairy-tale weddings. She didn't dare look at their friends. Their cheers followed them. Graciella felt carefree and lighter than she'd ever felt. All the burdens and trauma faded in comparison to her newfound happiness.

She never knew what peace was but being in Boss's arms, married to him, there was no way life could be any more perfect.

Graciella had found her soul mate and she was never going to give him up, not ever.

The End

www.samcrescent.com

www.staceyespino.com

EVERNIGHT PUBLISHING ®

www.evernightpublishing.com

www.ingramcontent.com/pod-product-compliance
Lightning Source LLC
Chambersburg PA
CBHW071306130626
46556CB00004B/1488